THE LEGACY SERIES

The Path of Totality
Marie Zhuikov

Shocker in Gloomtown
Dan Libman

The Continental Divide
Bob Johnson

The Three Devils and Other Stories
William Luvaas

The Correct Response
Manfred Gabriel

Welcome Back to the World: A Novella & Stories
Rob Davidson

Grayhound Cowboy and Other Stories
Ken Post

Close Call
Kim Suhr

The Waterman
Gary Schanbacher

Signs of the Imminent Apocalypse and Other Stories
Heidi Bell

What We Might Become
Sara Reish Desmond

The Silver State Stories
Michael Darcher

An Instinct for Movement
Michael Mattes

The Machine We Trust
Tim Conrad

Gridlock
Brett Biebel

Salt Folk
Ryan Habermeyer

The Commission of Inquiry
Patrick Nevins

Maximum Speed
Kevin Clouther

Reach Her in This Light
Jane Curtis

The Spirit in My Shoes
John Michael Cummings

The Effects of Urban Renewal on Mid-Century America and Other Crime Stories
Jeff Esterholm

What Makes You Think You're Supposed to Feel Better
Jody Hobbs Hesler

Fugitive Daydreams
Leah McCormack

Hoist House: A Novella & Stories
Jenny Robertson

Finding the Bones: Stories & A Novella
Nikki Kallio

In sharp, stunning prose, Diane Josefowicz captures the aching loneliness of childhood and its lasting impact on our struggle for connection. These eleven stories transport us through asylums, schools, burn units, and beyond, revealing the quiet strangeness of family and all the "aching effort" that makes a life.

—REBEKAH BERGMAN
author of *The Museum of Human History*

Diane Josefowicz's *Guardians & Saints* is a surreal story collection about people behaving badly. Mocking each other, laughing inappropriately, literally throwing punches, Josefowicz's characters act out everywhere, from orphanages for dead children, to strange family therapy sessions, to tense PTA meetings. Yet these bad actors are surprisingly moving. Gorgeously written, this is a melancholy, funny, deeply humane book about people transcending their own worst selves.

—KIM MAGOWAN
author of *Don't Take This the Wrong Way*

In *Guardians & Saints*, everyone is, in some sense, an orphan—unrooted, unparented, cursed to spend their lives searching for footing, healing, and home. The characters inhabit rickety families and the institutions that replace them: asylums, hospitals, schools. While the stories range from contemporary realism to more fantastical narratives, a fairy-tale mood pervades them all. Her stories remind us that enchantment is not necessarily a good thing, and that unloved children grow into adults who can never settle and feel safe. Marked by prose that makes the ordinary strange and dangerous. these unsettling, addictive tales are haunting in the best sense.

—EILEEN KELLY
author of *Small Wonder*

GUARDIANS & SAINTS

stories

DIANE JOSEFOWICZ

CORNERSTONE PRESS
UNIVERSITY OF WISCONSIN-STEVENS POINT

Cornerstone Press, Stevens Point, Wisconsin 54481
Copyright © 2025 Diane Josefowicz
www.uwsp.edu/cornerstone

Printed in the United States of America by
Point Print and Design Studio, Stevens Point, Wisconsin

Library of Congress Control Number: 2025943467
ISBN: 978-1-968148-09-6

This is a work of fiction. Names, characters, businesses, places, events, and incidents are either the products of the author's imagination or used in a fictitious manner. Any resemblance to actual persons, living or dead, or actual events is purely coincidental.

Cornerstone Press titles are produced in courses and internships offered by the Department of English at the University of Wisconsin–Stevens Point.

DIRECTOR & PUBLISHER
Dr. Ross K. Tangedal

EXECUTIVE EDITORS
Jeff Snowbarger, Freesia McKee

EDITORIAL DIRECTOR
Brett Hill

SENIOR EDITORS
Paige Biever, Eva Nielsen, Reilly Crous

PRESS STAFF
Lilly Kulbeck, Alex Diaz, Abby Paulsen, Samantha Bjork, Sophie McPherson, Madison Schultz, Autumn Vine

For my teachers

stories

The Dwindling

"Early stages in a Dwindling's rehabilitation are the most difficult, because there is invariably so little with which to work."

—*The Book of Querque: A Compendium of Advice for Pedagogues*

"WATCH THAT STEP," Dr. Querque warns, shouldering open the door that fronts his Home for Dwindling Boys and Girls. In the foyer, a trio of woodwork angels clasp psalters to their chests as they raise their bulging eyes to heaven. Their mouths are burnished Os.

"The threshold," he informs me, his words falling like other, lesser angels, from the dark height of his mouth, "is not what it used to be."

I follow, mindful of my fingers, which are grimed with the train's soot and beneath that, like a memory, dust from my mother's pencil sharpener. Emptying it was the last task she set me, keeping her expectations low, so I might easily exceed them and not burden her with a need for correction. Unlike my mother, Querque seems unfazed by what I require in this department. Of my belongings, I was allowed only my drafting compass, which Querque confiscated after he caught me using it to jimmy our compartment's lock. "Thus does the personality gain in structure, brick by brick," he said, straightening the lapels of his jacket, which gave off an odor of gingersnaps, though there were no such wonders on him.

(While he dozed, I checked.) This, too, was a lesson: Beware the senses, which bamboozle. An empty stomach, however, is incontestable. My last meal was yesterday.

I shrug myself from my coat, which Querque takes with no sign of the displeasure I am expecting, since I have been for some minutes dripping on his parquet. I shuck my good shoes, and my toes emerge, quivering shrimps, through holes that I swear to heaven weren't there before. Against the world's disorder, which eddies about me like a patch of bad water, all I can do is repeat my mother's advice: Stand straight, smile bright. *And hold.* Sensing my beaming has a bit of the beam about it (as my mother would say), I force my grimace into a less ersatz grin, as if for a photograph, and wait for the flash. There is no flash. Rummaging in the closet, Querque has not noticed my distress and, with luck, he won't.

He exchanges his raincoat for a smoking jacket of gray velveteen, not omitting to transfer my compass to the inside pocket. His ginger scent yields to a closet odor of damp wool and insecticide. Blocking the hallway's meager light, he is pale and narrow as a celery stalk: fibrous, wholesome, and just as hard to swallow. His velveteen jacket shares the sea's oily sheen.

Clunk! The door shuts, the bolt leaps home. I shift my feet to hide my toes and widen my smile until it is big enough to contain every last thing I never did for my mother. Querque averts his eyes.

MY MOTHER, the artist Helen Dando of New Bedford, claimed to be a reincarnation of Helen of old, and most days she did seem capable of launching anything, from the boats that took my father and returned him to us shining with fish scales, his pockets jangling with bounty, coin and shell, to the flotilla of toy tugboats that nightly went wheeling round the tub drain. Even the tide came and went at her behest, or so it seemed to me, leaving pewter puddles in which I found sea treasures: ropes of kelp that slimed through my fingers; tiny cowries that I threaded into bracelets; and best of all, lumps of sea glass, edges blunted by sand and water, my mother's elements. Every weekday, from September to June, I was propelled onto the school bus with a push of my mother's hand. I felt its impress on my back in the form of a gritty rash that oozed the whole time my father was away and dried up when he returned.

Father was a sailor. He set forth when my mother permitted it, but everything else about him was completely irregular, including his front tooth, which had been chipped, he told me, on a sea glass bottle. He presented me with a shard of the original which I promptly bit, cracking my incisor to match his. "Don't listen to anyone who tells you the apple never falls far from the tree," he advised as I, wincing, held his sea-scented handkerchief to my mouth. "The apple *never* falls. Count on it, small fry: we're always, already *redeemed*." When he was home, what he said seemed true. I was happy in a way that thrust the rest of my life, before and after his appearances, into shadow. But during the unsettled months of his absence, the natural order of trees and apples was inverted: It was as if he had fallen away from me.

It would be simple to say that I missed him, but that skeletal description will not do: The fact is, his absence shattered me, so that I was engulfed by a mood as heavy and shifting as the sand that held my mother's bronzes, her angels and demons, when she cast them. My father wouldn't stay in one place long enough for a pearl of belief in him to form in the nacre of my mind. Whereas my mother, who did not merely accept this state of affairs but abetted it, felt that the solicitation of a child's belief in the regularity of events to be an inexcusable seduction. But of course—and here I smile brighter, wider, *hold*—the point is not to cast blame or assign responsibility in retrospect, when nothing can be done. My father's changeability was probably constitutional. A sailor, he was always leaving. He would always go. This quirk suited my mutable mother—but it did not suit me. I dwindled, growing small and quiet. My mother took me to the doctor who, after pinching my wrist, pressing his stethoscope against my chest, and closing my eyelids with his fingers, prescribed my delivery to Querque.

"No!" I cried. I didn't want to leave my mother; above all I did not want to cede my chair by the window where I would sit drawing perfect circles with my compass while I kept an eye on the harbor, where my father's ship might arrive at any time.

That night, my mother dressed me in my fancy night-gown, stretched me out on the parlor's horsehair sofa, and swaddled me in a sheet. She placed coins on my eyes, as was her practice, to eliminate the dark circles she found so unattractive; and she reminded me, by way of a lullaby, that my father's perpetual departure was something I could rely on, as I could rely on the regular rearrangement of the night sky. She pointed at the window, through which Orion was just visible, wheeling around the pole star with his limbs forever locked, akimbo. "Not to worry," she sighed, covering the clock with a filmy black scarf. "All troubles go in the fullness of time." An electric glance over her shoulder: "Which, for you, is about as full as it gets." Querque's Home would be good for me, she added as she adjusted my lace collar. Her fingers drifted to my mouth, which she smoothed into a smile—wide, bright, and for a moment, held. At Querque's, she explained, I would at last understand my father's lesson. Even if I never stopped dwindling, at least I'd learn to come and go.

It is hard to say, in fact, what I will learn at the Home. For the moment, I am expected simply to do as I am told, and so commanded, I follow Querque down one corridor, and then another, until we arrive in a kitchen so brightly lit I wince.

From the ceiling, frying pans hang in rows, arranged by size and scoured to a dull luster. On the wall, knives cling to metal strips in order of ascending lethality: pare, slice, bone, hack, cleave. The tile floor's chill rises through the soles of my feet; a different chill descends down my arms. Though this room is a hymn to the attractive idea that stomachs are made for filling, I don't want to be scoured shiny. I don't want to wash my hands.

The tiled floor centers on a mosaic: a man dives from a platform into a river filled with dolphins. The far shore is gold. Presiding over everything is a graying woman whose pince-nez dangles from a chain.

"Lunette Bicky," Querque says, "meet our newest appointment, Monday One-Thirty."

If I ever had another name, it has been lost in Querque's pockets, along with my compass.

Squinting, Lunette regards me with her dominant eye. At the center of her gunmetal irises, the pupils have contracted to pinheads. "You couldn't find a Tuesday, or a Sunday?"

"As you know, Lunette," Querque sniffs, "there are only so many days in the week, and so many hours in the day."

"There are exactly seven," she retorts, "and twenty-four, respectively. As *you* know."

Lunette spins on her heel. Dr. Querque gives me a push not unlike my mother's school bus propulsions and disappears like a startled smelt. I must have gasped because Lunette troubles herself to reassure me: "Never mind. You'll get to know his little ways."

She hands me a homemade lollipop, not quite round and slightly soft. As I tongue it, a headache blooms behind my eyes. Sugar is not allowed at home. I thrust the lollipop into my pocket.

"You are more a chips-and-pickle sort of girl," she observes.

Despite my suspicions about Querque and his Home for Dwindlers, I find myself warming to this Lunette Bicky.

"I was a naturalist in the former life," Lunette says.

"What's that?"

She tilts her head. "Don't you know?"

Instead of answering, I roll something sticky between my fingertip and the countertop.

"Let me show you around," she says, lifting my hand and swiping under it with a rag. "You have a lot to learn. And," she sniffs, tipping my chin to peer briefly into my eyes, "only me to teach you."

"What do you mean?"

"Never mind, you'll know soon enough." She's halfway across the kitchen before I can say another word. "Come along."

In the pantry—described with special emphasis as *off-limits*—Lunette shows me canisters of oatmeal, baking powder and cornstarch, tinned peaches and sardines. Among the cookbooks, I recognize one with an embossed spine: *TUTTI FRUTTI DI MARE*. My mother, who had a copy, translated the title for me: All the fruits of the sea. That was as much as I learned from it, though, because my father, whose seafaring meant months of nothing but fish in the belly, preferred turf to surf while at home, and so the book gathered dust while my mother griddled hamburgers that, despite her acquiescence to my father's wish, nevertheless tasted faintly of kelp, as if she could never give up the sea entire. Here, too, rules seem sustained by resistance: Although the typewriter, shining with polish, is not to be touched, Lunette opens a drawer to show me where she keeps her supplies, tiny screwdrivers for making repairs and extra ribbons, as if to suggest that someday I might have the privilege of requiring them. So far, at Querque's, I've been given exactly nothing (unless you count the lollipop) yet still, this Lunette Bicky holds things before me—sweets, pickles, hopes.

Tacked to the door is a chart that I mistake at first for a picture of sea coral, delicate outgrowths branching from a sturdy trunk.

"Is that the limbic system?" Something of which my mother had often spoken, in tones of awe.

"Limbo, more like." Her tolerant smile stops at her eyes.

"The dance?" I shimmy, to show that I know exactly what she means.

"Welcome to our Home," Lunette says, in a tone that ends my clowning. "That picture is a food tree." Yet her explanation explains nothing. Only fruit and nuts grow on trees, not milk or meat. Why does "merengue" appear at the base of the trunk, why is "spaghetti" an afterthought scribbled at the tip of an otherwise unelaborated branch, and what in this topsy-turvy universe of aliment is a "clam tongue," and for what does a clam need a tongue anyway?

She tacks the day's meal plan to the door.

TODAY'S LUNCH:

Suey, American chop, and
Bread, white, sandwich, sliced, with
Apples, peeled, various and
Milk, skim, cold, in cups.

I am staring at a spool of correction tape when Lunette mutters, "Well, he doesn't like *everything* I cook."

The Dictum of Light: As the outside shapes the inside, so bright environments beget those angels known as happy children. But, to keep utility bills down, turn off lights *religiously*.

Monday dawns, but only just. The sun, abashed, fingers the horizon before withdrawing behind a thundercap so gray and heavy it might have been cut from Querque's smoking jacket. Over breakfast, rain drips into my oatmeal. I move to a drier spot and spoon what I can into my mouth. When I am finished, Lunette exchanges my bowl for a vegetable peeler and directs me to the kitchen where my morning task is already laid out, in the form of a colander of indifferently washed fingerling potatoes. They refuse to be skinned without a struggle that eventuates in the peeling of exactly five fingerlings and part of one finger. I wrap a rag around the wound *and hold*. But the scab lacks all conviction, and I am without recourse, for Lunette, who has the morning off, is the only one who knows where to find the first-aid kit. Lunch is leftover oatmeal, sticky as the Band-Aid I am not wearing. The first bite clots in my throat. I spit it into a napkin and toss it all in the trash so the problem it represents may belong to some other metabolic process, to someone else's future. Mine is already sealed, in the form of this afternoon's Session with Querque.

At twenty minutes past the hour, I arrive in the waiting room. Nothing happens when I switch on the lamp. Pulling the chain only deepens the cut on my finger. In the gloom I take deep breaths; I repeat, sotto voce, the Dictum of Light; I leaf through a magazine called *Emphases—Fun Has No Purpose*. (The masthead reveals that this is also one of Querque's publications; its logo is a stylized reproduction of the diver I saw on the kitchen floor.) I press my injured finger against the upholstery until my dubious scab makes a pinprick stain. The curtains are the same graphite-colored velveteen as Querque's jacket; on the window side, they are lined with watered silk, also gray.

The door opens. I rise and offer my hand to Querque, who sees my finger and recoils. I ignore him—*straight, bright, hold!*—and cross the threshold, brushing my undamaged fingers on the jamb, enameled in a pale gray that matches Querque's pallor as well as the bluish half-moons that have lately appeared at the base of each of my fingernails. The room is long and narrow, with a stone fireplace brimful of books at one end. Against one wall, a pressboard desk sags under the weight of several piles of *The Book of Querque*, still in their plastic wrapping. My nose prickles, registering a shift in Querque's peculiar atmosphere, the omnipresent ginger now mixed with ink. Over the mantel, there's a painting: a pale child sprawls on a makeshift bed in a dark cottage. Her parents stand in a shadowed corner, while an old man sits beside her in a cone of lamplight, his chin propped in his hand as if he is considering a tricky problem in long division. When I try to shut the door behind me, it swings open again, as if obeying some secret imperative of Querque's.

Or perhaps my mother, exercising her talent for action-at-a-distance, has bewitched the catch.

Querque turns a bolt high on the door. "Old houses," he says, and shakes his head.

"Yes," I say, taking a seat as far as possible from the maroon recliner that occupies the room's center. Beside it, on the coffee table, brown eggs nestle in a woven basket beside a lit candle and a pad of yellow legal paper.

Querque folds himself like a stork into the recliner.

"My mother—"

"Caskets vouchsafed to the deepest deep," he intones. "Sea burials, small fry."

Instead of the door, it is my breath that catches. He sounds just like my father.

"Your father is not the issue."

Our eyes meet. And hold. Now I know what I am dealing with. My mother was a mind-reader, too—one of her talents, like sending people away, calling them back.

"First things first." I am not looking at his mouth, only his eyes—a trick I learned from my mother. It is like listening to a statue talk. The slate quality of his irises suffuses his whole being. "*Your* name is Monday."

"No, it's not," I mutter, and cross my arms over my chest.

"This stiffness will fade in time," he informs me as he hands me a tissue. "That's a nasty cut you've got there, by the way. Blot the seepage, there's a girl. Now, to resume. You are Monday One-Thirty. Of course, you are not limited to your scheduled appointment."

I twist the tissue around my bleeding finger, and fist my left hand damply into my right. "Where is my father?"

He makes a note in his yellow legal pad.

"*Where is my—*"

"You've come a long way," he interrupts, "and now you've been found."

"Like a foundling?" I am making a joke to obscure the fact that I don't understand, but Querque presses his lips together so they turn pale like the rest of him.

"Like a *dwindling*."

He takes an egg from the bowl at his elbow and holds it before the flame. Through the shell, I see the outline of the yolk and inside it, something curled like a fiddlehead fern. The fetal chick: unborn, perhaps unbearable. He returns the egg to the basket and pinches the candle's wick. Acrid smoke twists up my nose.

"The tree fell away from you. Such things happen."

Querque's tone, which seems intended to comfort, seizes me with anxiety instead. Mother's pencils will need sharpening, her teapot warming, her roughened hands their weekly liniment. Hadn't I proven myself useful? I had, I *know* it, the way I know my multiplication tables, the way I once knew my own name. Soon—very soon—she will realize her mistake.

"I trust Lunette has gone over the house rules. I am particular about locks and closets, as she no doubt has told you. You may not enter the pantry without permission, and the basement is expressly not your affair unless you are working at the loom." His tone, which has been strict, softens. "But my door is always open to you, Monday."

Overhead, the bulb expires with a snap.

"Oh, these old houses!" Twin pink spots appear on Querque's cheeks. "Please, do excuse the light."

In the half-dark, he removes his glasses and rubs where they have left angry blotches on either side of his nose. Now there's soot as well—two symmetrical smudges that might stand for anything that unites with a contrary: life and death, mother and father, egg and sperm.

Reality and dream.

I blush.

"You've no idea," he mutters, aiming his words toward the expired ceiling light, "what it takes to run this place."

Of course, I have no idea. Although I recoil from this glimpse into his private universe of home economics, of dead bulbs and decrepit electrical systems—not to mention the thankless edification of children—I am pleased by the bit of trust he's placed in me. Surely Querque does not make *all* his charges privy to his frustrations. His disclosure also suggests that the Home is a more reassuring place than I'd imagined, involving no witchcraft, none of my mother's sea skullduggery—and no maritime adventuring, either. Which, I admit, is a relief.

He fixes me with his cool gaze like a bit of sea wrack pinned to a board, a look that tells me I would be quite wrong to infer anything from his lapse of decorum about the light.

"Let us review. Your name is?"

"Muh," I stammer. "Muh-muh-muh."

A human noise, dwindling. Querque smiles.

"That's the magic," he says, "of the right name. It calls you out. An in-voc-ay-tion."

But I mean: The one I left. The one who left me. His stone irises twist in their veined settings. I flash on a memory of the market, where I once saw the butcher pull an eyeball dripping from the head of a freshly killed ox. My mother hurried me away before I could see what he did with the other one. "All that showing off," she sniffed, "just to put dinner on the table. The prehistory of an oxtail soup is all it is. No need to glorify it with a performance."

I shove my shredded tissue into my pocket where it will stick to the remains of Lunette's lollipop.

"Say something, Monday. You are a naughty oyster withholding its pearl."

"Muh." One syllable. How many oysters contain more than one pearl?

"Try again. You can do it."

"*Mutt*," I conclude, letting my tongue touch the roof of my mouth. What a revelation, to let anything touch anything else. I tingle all over, hot and cold at once, a single tap through which opposing impulses roar. Yet hadn't my tongue been in my mouth all along? Perhaps the butcher's ox was just a dream.

"Mutton," Querque sighs. His stomach squeals. Mutton had once been a patient, perhaps. Was she turned into a soup? At any rate, he's got *me* pegged: My appetite has always been a problem. I glorify imaginary soup, and reject real lollipops, even when someone puts one in my hand.

"Mutt," I croak, to recall Querque from his lambchop reverie. Already I want to mean more to him than Mutton, whoever *she* is. Was. "Mutt, mutt, MUTT!"

Dr. Querque's eyes flick in their sockets—a torpid, reptilian look.

Is—*was?*—that my heart?

"Good girl."

> The Axiom of Perfection: Nothing's made that's not first dreamed *with great precision.* Thus, to make a perfect child, pour equal parts sweet and dry vermouth over ice. The perfection of the result will depend on the exactness of your measurements.

We number twenty—ten boys, ten girls—and range in age from seven to twelve. At ten apiece, Fobb and I form a kind of hinge, with equal numbers of older and younger children arrayed on either side of us, like wings. It is not much, but it is enough to cement a friendship, of sorts.

The day begins with Washing Up. On cold mornings we punch the washbowl's scrim of ice before sluicing ourselves wide-awake and shivering. Breakfast in the dining hall is porridge, coffee, sometimes milk. Lunette administers the first of three daily doses of Happiness Elixir, which I swallow penitentially, mouthfuls of scummed lake. After breakfast, we take turns using the Happy Lights, a row of large boxes that emit a bluish glow in which we are each expected to bask for thirty minutes. Next comes Useful Work: vegetable peeling, sweep-and-mop, polishing the foyer's woodwork angels. In the kitchen, we learn the infinite and various divisibility of food: chop, julienne, dice, mince, slice. Lunch is whatever Lunette dreams into existence at her typewriter, followed by more Elixir. Each afternoon has its own special task: *Looming*, in which we work the Home's basement loom, spooling out lengths of gray velveteen; *Foraging*, in which we gather mushrooms from the woods, or wild chives, according to Lunette's whim and the day's menu; and *Group*, which involves sitting in a circle and complaining about each other while Lunette looks on and occasionally dispenses advice, a reprimand, or just some mysterious proverb like "It don't rain—but it do, it do," "No good deed goes unpolished," or, my favorite, "Mind your peas—*and* your queues." The older children are also required to *Leaflet*, a task that involves distributing pamphlets about the Home to passersby. What Querque grandly calls our "literature" are only saddle-stitched Xerox pages stuck with a card that gives Querque's contact information, his official headshot—in which he wears a slight smile and the everlasting velveteen coat—and the Home's slogan in large serif:

DR. QUERQUE'S HOME FOR DWINDLERS. WE'LL FINISH THEM OFF SO YOU DON'T HAVE TO! As I distribute pamphlets, I stand straighter, smile brighter—all that time before the Happy Lights must shine through my eyes, and my chipped tooth should be a beacon, just in case one of the women on the street happens to be my mother. She never is. Even so, I press my leaflets on everyone, but with less enthusiasm as the weeks pass.

As my enthusiasm flags, my guilt increases, until I am sure that my mother did not forsake me. Rather, *I* was the one who abandoned *her*. A sin for which I am sure to be punished: Despite raging hunger, I eat only morsels and I say nothing for days at a time, the better to insure my invisibility, which conveniently both confers protection and punishes me in advance.

This perversity is why, once a week, like everyone else I have a *Session with Querque.*

Sometimes Lunette will assign a special task, like spider collector or hedgerow trimmer—a job that Fobb got once, and lost again almost immediately, for he used the cleaver to slice the tail off the neighbor's pig. He offered it to Lunette, who cuffed him, and sent me across the yard with a dollar and a typed apology, which I dropped into a puddle so that it turned into a robin and flew away. I was sure I would receive a scolding, but when I skulked back to the kitchen Lunette was by the hearth, seizing the tail in a bright fire. She waved me over and offered me a bite. My mouth ran with juice, and for a moment I nearly remembered my name.

At other times, Lunette equips us with shovels and buckets and sends us to the beach to dig up clams that she steams, reserving the liquid for the next batch of Elixir.

Only Querque is allowed to answer the phone.

When we play the Name Game, Fobb starts us off, waving Lunette's broom as we circle the butcher block, slipping on the tiles.

Fobb menaces a fish-faced girl with the broom.

How do you say his name?

The point is to reply before someone touches you and makes you It.

"You say it like murky!" She skitters away, laughing. "Murky" is one of the easy answers.

Fobb nears; I duck into the pantry.

"Jerky!" Screamed by a boy who wears headgear all night long to straighten his overbite.

Fobb toes open the pantry door and locks eyes with me.

HOW DO YOU SAY HIS NAME?

Murky. Jerky. "Tetrazzini turkey!" I shout, in my excitement setting a row of pans clanging with my elbow. Lunette materializes, summoned by our noise.

"Children," she says, shooing us, "are a lot of work."

Later, a batch of Happy Crackers crisps in the oven, filling the house with such an atmosphere of molasses that I abandon my post at the loom. In the kitchen, Lunette roosts on a stool, shelling peas.

"Lunette," I muse, rolling her name in my wet mouth as I root in the sink, looking for the molasses spoon, which surely has not been washed yet. "That's a lovely monocle."

"Monocle de mon oncle," she quips, smiling as she adjusts her pince-nez, which even I know has nothing to do with a monocle. "In other words, don't be ridiculous."

"I *shall* be ridiculous." I love how she speaks, how she smiles, how she sits and shells her peas. I sidle over, the molasses spoon wholly forgotten. Lunette flicks her towel— *no, no*—but I am too fast. The stolen pea tastes *green*, the greenest green imaginable: I am eating a beanfield, a pine forest, a thicket of holly. Lunette eyes me, and I grin, a green grin, one that is not bright or straight but lets her know that I am happy even though she says words, like *mon oncle*, that I don't understand.

Attracted by the tiled floor's diver, I plop down beside him and push a runaway pea into the grout, greening it to match my tongue, which must be green as a meadow by now.

"Tsk," she clucks. "Don't make work."

"I miss my mother," I murmur to the squished pea.

Lunette grabs a towel. Two swipes and the pea is gone, a mess I never made. She folds the towel just so and hangs it on the oven door. A tile dolphin smiles at me and flits away.

"Lunette, I miss my mother!" I am wailing. Querque has warned me about this, how easily my moods monsoon me.

"Get off the floor," Lunette commands. She sets me on a stool and looks me straight in the eye. "Nobody ever wants it to end the way it did." Lunette's face is sweet and sour, the one combination I am completely unable to resist. "But all things end, all the time. Still we roll, like beans in a bottle. Just like your daddy. We roll all round the world."

Tears spurt from me, even as Lunette's expression hardens. This is as much genuine instruction as anyone has yet given me here at the Home, and no one except Querque has ever mentioned my father, or even considered that I might have one. My breathing is ragged, as if my lungs are being sliced like loaves. Perhaps that is why the Home is so austere, why even Lunette's eyes at times remind me of nothing so much as the knives on the wall. Kindness, if it exists at all, is a blade—and it is serrated. Could children die of it? I don't recall if this problem is addressed in the *Book of Querque*.

"I leave the question," Querque concludes, "as an exercise for the reader."

> The Axiom of Soup: When upset, the typical Dwindler boils over, *comme une soupe au lait*. When things cool down, the result is always the same: a thin skin and a lingering odor.

Querque is such a busy man! He has so many responsibilities, he can never take a vacation. For without him, what would become of us? Who would walk the Home Boundary, checking for intrusions? Who would reminds us to swallow our doses of Elixir, to Do Useful Work, to Take Exercise, to worship at our Happy Lights? Who would make all those notes in the special yellow pads, writing down all the forgettable things we say? And who would punish us for infractions, like talking out of turn or clamming up in session, sneaking to the quays instead of having a Soothing Snack? Our mothers, we repeat from *The Book of Querque*, did their best, but we would be too much for anyone.

What is the proof? At night, in dreams, we're too much, even, for ourselves.

"Mermaids!"

"Giant squid!"

"No-eyed sole!"

News of these and other wonders filters from bed to bed in whispers after lights-out. We dream in unison, drifting on drafts of sleep, each colder than the last, until we reach the deepest deep. In the morning, the unity of our slumber shatters with the crusts that fall from our eyes as we take our turns at the washbowl, the shock of an elbow jammed into the ribs as we spill down the stairs. At times, in the night, I sense a presence by my bed. Although in the morning I am sure it was only Lunette, coming to check on me, in my sleep, I shiver, and dream of long division.

One night, the dormitory buzzes with a different rumor, as fantastic in its way as mermaids or one-eyed sole: Once upon a time, Querque had a wife! Her name was Friday Last. That no one has actually seen her only serves to further stimulate our humming collective imagination. She is said to be a ghost, and to wear, variously, jodhpurs, a gray velveteen tracksuit, or a porkpie hat; she prunes the orchard at midnight, leaving tiny apples all around, and sometimes rattles the pans in the kitchen. The younger children say she popped from his head like Athena; and sure enough, over his right eyebrow, there is a small scar. Or else she sprang from notes on Querque's yellow legal pad, making her the sum of our remarks. Which, in point of fact—or more precisely, fancy—she most likely is, which is why I suffer my shameful fantasies of Mutton in absolute silence. (I confess her name bothers me terribly. Surely, in moments of passion, Querque must call her something else. Lambchop?) As usual, Fobb has a different take: He whispers that once upon a time, this mythological wife was a real Dwindling like us, a girl by the name of Monday-At-Four, and that she was my clone in all but my sex.

I've changed a lot since coming to the Home, but I'm still a girl as far as I know. I smooth the rough blanket down over my chest and hips. "My sex?"

"Which is thus far indeterminate," he sneers.

It is true: I am as yet unhipped, unbreasted. Fobb makes such mischief. With one offhand remark, I am overwhelmed with envy. If only I had more to eat, if only the dormitory were not so cold. I burrow under my insufficient covers, pulling the blanket over my ears in order to block out Fobb's giggling. As for Friday Last: I hate her.

One afternoon the phone rings in the hallway, where I am polishing the angels, but Querque is nowhere to be found. To be sure he's not on the stoop, I heave the front door open, and an idea arrives: That is my mother, *my mother*, on the line! The wind picks up, so fresh it might have blown my father back from the sea; I mean, it carries the same conviction, the same odor of iron and salt. Yet to answer the phone is expressly forbidden and I have no idea what sort of punishment I might incur. No one, to my knowledge, has ever dared so much naughtiness under Querque's roof.

The ringing stops. I rub lemon polish into an angel's mouth until it squeaks. After months of Elixir, Group, and

Sessions with Querque, all that remains of my mother is the memory of her kitchen, sharded with gray sea light. *Stand straight! Smile bright!* I sink through a fug of lemon-polish. The angels shine: *O, O, O.*

Elixir time! Lunette comes with the bottle, her pocket bristling with scoured spoons. I drag myself from the floor and follow her into the kitchen where I swallow my dose without a thought in my head.

"A good cry helps sometimes," Lunette says, peering into my mouth. Her suspicions are unnecessary; in six months I have come a long way from my days of wincing and spitting up. She must have heard me sobbing in the foyer. She moves on to Fobb, who takes his medicine, or appears to, but before she can check he ducks away. All at once I understand: He is not grinning because the Elixir is working but because he knows it is a lie.

Lunette regards Fobb as if he were a son whose future was less than assured.

And whose fault is that, I ask Querque the next day. Or I try to, anyway. My mouth opens and closes but no sound comes out.

"Be bold, be bold!" Querque is in an expansive mood. His velveteen jacket has a feathery luster and underneath, he wears a bright red sweater, an ensemble that makes him look just like the robin that carried off Lunette's apology.

He frowns. If he is a robin, I might be a worm.

"Well, not *too* bold," he says, looking at me sidelong. "Some faults are basic, like fissures in the earth. Death Valley has quite a few of them. Thus the name."

"The name."

"You are still angry about your name."

At once, I seethe. I am about to become that dreaded pedagogical catastrophe, the terrible *soupe au lait*. If I ever cool down, a smelly skin will replace my own, and no one will whisper to me anymore after lights-out. Yet I hadn't known

I was angry until he said I was, which makes no sense at all. I shake my head to dispel the hiss that has invaded it, the final warning before I boil over. To let off steam, I complain about Lunette:

"Why won't Lunette brush my hair?"

"It is too tempting to smack you with the brush."

"Why won't she run the bath?"

"It is too tempting to drown you."

"And the ironing?"

"Again, a temptation. Aren't you avoiding something?"

"How so?" I'm confused. "I thought she loved me."

"*Loves* you? Think, Monday. The hot iron, your young skin."

Which smells slightly off. Unless the odor is coming from that dirty hovel, the one in the painting that hangs over the book-filled fireplace. The father rests his hand on the mother's shoulder as she sobs into the crook of her arm. The lampshade is askew. Such noise, such disorder, such insufficient light—

"What is it, Monday?"

From the plate I pick the last Happy Cracker, only to set it down again.

"Is she dead?" I wonder, pointing to the painting.

He sets down his yellow legal pad: "We have to stop."

"*Is she dead?*"

"That will be all, Monday."

I reach for something solid, a cockle shell, a lump of sea glass. My hand closes over a palmful of air.

> The Axiom of Slumber: Regiment sleep as every-thing else—enough to ensure productivity, but not so much that your charges are tumbled into promiscuous dreams. Excessive contact with this realm will only distract them from their new reality.

At the sink, Lunette washes up under water so hot her hands turn the scalded pink of the pigs' heads I've seen piled at the market, their white-lashed eyes shut forever against us, because they have seen too much of the things we do out of our bottomless need: our failures to attend Session, take our Elixir, use our Lights.

"I've just been to the butcher's," Lunette announces, apparently unaware of the crimson dots on her velveteen apron. One of Fobb's mischiefs, I conclude, at the loom.

"I'm sorry he called you a swine, Lunette," Fobb replies, not missing a beat.

"Filthy, filthy." Lunette shakes her hands dry and the droplets fly off like diamonds, like stars. Querque would insist that I choose—*Choice is what made you human,* he repeats, until I want to bark, to howl, to chitter like a bat, all at once—but I can't. I want those water droplets to be both diamonds and stars; above all, I want the water to be something other than what it is: nasty, Querquefied water that has been embittered by its journey through Querque's nasty pipes.

These days, I hate Querque with all my heart, and I love Lunette with equal intensity.

"Pigs are smart," I offer, wrung out with longing. "They have big brains."

"And curly tails!" Fobb pulls my pigtail. I make a grab for him, but he is too fast. As he skips from the room, he flings something long and sinuous against the far wall. It drops to the tiles, then slithers beneath a gap in the molding. I put my hands to my head. Has my hair turned to snakes? The knives fall in a bright clatter that makes Lunette curse. I bite my lip in order to have a better reason to cry.

"Head cheese," she says, when she has replaced the last blade, a demilune mincer that cuts scallions to ribbons as thin as she has lately become. "Sweetbreads."

This is not the reprimand I am expecting, for having provoked Fobb to yet another mischief. *Sweetbreads,* I repeat, under my breath. A word that is exactly what it says, sweet and satisfying in my mouth. But I am on Carb Control. No sweets, no bread. Querque doesn't like dense girls. *Starvation resets the system.* So it is writ, in *The Book of Querque.*

That night, when I stick my legs under the covers, the sheet stops at my ankles. I twist free of the bedclothes, kicking against the current that threatens to pull me away.

"Settle down," Lunette growls from the corner where she rocks, knitting the blankets that cover us while we sleep, that protect us from the wind blowing in through the window. (Querque's dictum: Fresh air!)

I flop over, only to choke on a cloud of foul powder. Not only have I been short-sheeted, but my pillow has been turned into a flour sack. Fobb! The mischief-maker, the thief in the kitchen, the bad boy who sleeps by the door like an on-the-outs god.

"Back to bed!" Lunette's bark harries me down the corridor. A bony leg shoots out from the dark. I land on my rump. Tears and snot spurt from me. But before I can bawl, Fobb is there, his hand clapped over my mouth.

"Shh." Fobb, crouching, blows on my scraped palms, a tenderness that closes my throat. I pull my hands away and blow on them myself. He stands: "Follow me."

"Where are we going?"

"To the basement."

"But that's off-limits!"

"Come on."

In the basement Fobb has fixed the loom so that when he turns the crank, the velveteen that shoots out the other end bears a looping pattern that, on closer inspection, is a series of scrawled words. Bad ones, the kind my father and mother would exchange sometimes in the middle of the night when they, in their passion, were unmindful of my ears.

"Fobb!"

"Shh!"

Eyes shut, Fobb stands at the loom in a blind trance, skimming his palms over the fabric. "Say it loud, say it quick, everybody knows you're sick, sick, SICK!"

I dash away—up the stairs, out the back door, and down the street to the sea. It is a calm night, the sky dense with stars, and silent, apart from the regular brush of waves on the shore. Fobb arrives, breathing hard. We make our truce and explore the beach. When his back is turned, I throw a fistful of sand in his direction.

> The Axiom of Fasting: The longer the fast, the better the lesson is learned. Under consistently maintained conditions of near-starvation, your teachings will take on an abalone fastness, glittering and hard.

The next day, our foraging bears such an unusual quantity of *frutti di mare* that, at midday, we return with a whole bushel of tiny clams. Lunette turns them into dinner: Spaghetti, Vongole.

That evening, Fobb discovers in his spaghetti a clam that failed to open during Lunette's steaming. I must have missed it during prep. This how we know, Lunette says, frowning at me, that the clam is rotten.

Fobb tosses the bad clam up and down.

"Who's rotten?" I demand to know. I am out of sorts because of course, Lunette is right. The implication is obvious: I am that clam. It hits me between the eyes and lands in my spaghetti. Fobb whoops: Bulls-eye! I cry and cry.

"Spaghetti is nothing to cry about," Lunette consoles me. Her apron is a scrap from the loom. I recognize, with horror, the variegated pattern from the night that Fobb and I were down there. And her eyes, her eyes! are ringed with such darkness, all the nights I refused to sleep. "On second thought, maybe I should have butterflied a lamb."

Mutton's fate. My face is flaming, my tears are hot, but the rest of me goes cold as vichyssoise. "No, Lunette!"

"All this screaming, and for what? Wipe your eyes," she instructs me, handing me a napkin. It, too, is stenciled with obscenities that are apparently only visible to me. "And eat your dinner."

Her tone is bitter as the monarch to the bird who consumes it; this is what keeps the monarch safe. Numbly, I spoon clam broth into my mouth. I will never be so bitter. I will never be that safe.

During washing-up, the setting sun cinches the sky, shaping it up, notch by notch, on the way to the horizon. The dishwater roars down the drain, headed like everything else for the sea. I slip away, into the pantry, without a thought in my head beyond the usual, straight and bright. But the pantry is empty. Even Lunette's typewriter is gone. My compass, shining in the sunset that reflects off the glass cabinet panes, has been jabbed into the wall, where it holds up a sign: FEAST YOUR EYES—AND NOTHING ELSE!

The door creaks. Is it the monkey wind, my distant mother's craft, the woodwork angels at last finding their tongues?

"Monday?" Querque calls from beyond the threshold.

I brim and fizz, *une soupe au lait*. It takes only a moment to dislodge my compass, which I grip in my fist with the point turned out, thinking only to finish the job that butcher started. I'll take Fobb with me when I go; his naughtiness, after all, is what gets me through. Dusk breathes me in, straight and bright. Hold.

The Radio

MY FATHER, A PLAYWRIGHT, wrote exclusively for radio. The invisible medium appealed to his taste for infinite and empty spaces through which signals might propagate, uncorrupted, forever.

Writing for radio, Father worked within a space that was so remote, far fetched, and improbable that his most ardent admirers dubbed him His Acoustic and sent him tributes of sound: rare recordings of famous musicians, or libraries of unusual effects (fifteen renditions of a flushing toilet; twenty-five versions of a slamming car door). But it would be a mistake to say that such adulation alone motivated my father. His love for radio issued from a deeply seated preference (I should perhaps say *desire*) for disembodiment. When my father listened to radio plays, he was quite simply out of his mind. "Are you still on the planet, Annalise?" he would ask, after we'd listened to *War of the Worlds* for what seemed to my impatient child's mind the hundredth time. "Because I'm not, Annalise, not at all."

An Englishman born in fen country, my father was autochthonous and stalky as the local asparagus and, like the asparagus, he seemed to have poked straight up into the oozy landscape through a deep mulch of silt and ancestral bones. Reserved, solitary, and fastidious, Father was picky about his appearance: the cut of his trousers, the fabric's hand and drape. Quiet and careful of my grooming, I took after my father, listening to my tiny transistor alone in my room. My mother was a brassy American sociology professor whom my father had married in a fit of anti-British pique that was, according to Mother's dissertation, more British than anything else, or so he would tell me later, over cups of tea that he swallowed without enjoyment in a shadowy corner of the kitchen. Although the peculiarities of the British Male were something of a professional obsession for my mother, she abjured tea as a matter of principle and preferred coffee, with a dash of cream, which she thought was best consumed out in the big, busy world where she was noisy and astonishing—above all at the Faculty Club where she held court on Thursday afternoons.

Where Father was spare in every sense, Mother was voluptuous, her head crowned with a nimbus of hair so pale it was almost white; she had a rumbling voice and a fondness for home perms, plastic orchids, and rayon dresses—in other words, she was American to her peroxide roots, a fact that, for her, posed an urgent existential question. In contrast, Father's response to the question "So, where are you from?" was only dull incomprehension; for him, exile held no fascination, and migrations were for other people. What mattered was the condition of being anchored to the spot, a pitiless and pure collusion with gravity, the inescapability of which was leavened, however, by a few precious affordances: by day, there was the open prospect through the picture window; by night, the endless black sky which he called God's inkpot. And in which could be seen, as he told me every night when he tucked me into bed, the blaze of comets against a boot-blacked canvas, the doe-see-doe of Earth's endless promenade with the stars.

Mother's work took us back and forth across the Atlantic, and we never lived for more than a year or two in one place. But what I wish to write about is the brief time we spent in New Bedford, with its wharves and cobbled streets, its maritime museum full of scrimshaw and skeletons of whales. This year seems, in my memory, to extend toward a damp infinity in both directions, as if its drizzly gray atmosphere had somehow suffused everything I did and was, before and after, with a must of kelp and seawater.

The year we lived in New Bedford, my father took me on long walks along the docks where boats once floated full of whalebone and spermaceti. "Radio," Father would opine, clutching my hand as the gulls circled and screeched against the cloud-girdled sky, "happens in sound, but sound is not what matters about radio. No, what matters is the signal, absolute, intimate but untouchable, sensually charged but technically remote—and possibly deadly in its effects." He squeezed my hand so I would know he was teasing but it was too late, for I was already electric with fear, and shrank from him. He stared down at me for a moment, then grinned. "Mostly," he chuckled, "it's important to stage it correctly. Not to worry, this is a technical operation that leaves the ghosts alone. Annalise, we are artisans! All we must do is unfold a game of position between far-flung bodies, unknown to us and generally unknown to each other."

New Bedford was rainy, and Father rarely ventured outside without a yellow mackintosh and matching rubber boots. This display of sartorial practicality made him an instant hit with the locals. Bursting into the local tavern with water pouring from his close-cropped gray hair, he seemed as rough-hewn as any of them. Until he spoke, that is, and then his quiet voice exercised a further magic, for his plummy vowels and unvoiced r's suggested cultivation. No one was more surprised than my father when, upon expressing his admiration for a dish of stewed ay-pricots in a restaurant, he received an impromptu interview with the blushing dessert chef and a copy of the recipe printed on an index card, her phone number inscribed shyly at the bottom. "I doubt your mother would approve," he whispered as we walked out the door. "But voice is a kind of power."

ON AN EXCURSION to the shopping mall, my father and I passed an electronics shop. Something in the window seized Father's attention with such force that he dropped my hand and pointed. There, on a shelf above a dusty television, was a rectangular object somewhat larger than a mousetrap, of salmon Bakelite marbled with white. It sported a handful of screws and knobs and, in the center, a thimble-shaped dome of glass rested over what looked like a stone. Beside it stood a cardboard box, its printing faded, although set against a deep blue field the stylized yellow lightning still brightly framed the words: Philmore Super Radio Crystal Set.

Father pushed himself up on the balls of his feet and banged on the shop door. When it finally swung open, the air exploded with the sound of tiny bells.

The technician appeared then, smiling, and waved us in. Fluorescent bulbs lit the interior and the air stank of mildewed carpet and burnt plastic. All round us, on small tables and counters, were bits and pieces of electronic equipment: woofers and tweeters, cables with red and white termini, tubes from an old television, a milk crate full of transistor radios. The technician's white shirt was streaked with dark grease; his wide blue tie was none too clean, either.

"I notice you've a Philmore Super. Though I would say that cover's not original." My father's voice was sly.

The technician beamed. "I'm pleased to tell you the set is almost forty years old, sir. In *very* fine condition, considering how few have survived. "

"Flimsy, cheap, made for mass consumption," sighed my father with the aggrieved tone I recognized from certain conversations with my mother, usually conducted behind a locked door.

The technician retrieved the crystal wireless from the window and placed it on the counter, where he began to fiddle with a piece of wire that stuck out of the garish Bakelite, fine as a cat's whisker. A tinny voice insinuated itself into the room.

With the wind
in her butterscotch hair

Father harrumphed and raised both eyebrows, sure signs that he was impressed.

"I'll buy your wireless," he said, retrieving a pen from his pocket, "but let me show you what I *really* want."

He began to sketch on the back of the technician's receipt book. The technician came around and peered over his shoulder. Their conversation turned to the details of radio physics. If Father provided the specifications, would the technician make him a special kind of receiver, through which it might be possible to catch and amplify certain kinds of signals, for instance pulsar radiation, or radio waves pinging back from distant stars?

"Who nowadays could form, for example, a proper notion of the sound of the trumpets at Jericho? Lost voices, forgotten sounds, vibrations lock-stepping into the void and now too distant to ever be recaptured! The dead can only say so much. What sort of arrows could transfix such birds?"

"Yes!" cried the technician. "I have a little spark—"

"While the phonograph, for instance, reproduced sounds, it couldn't record an eloquent silence, or the voice of blood, or that of conscience!"

"Yet," the technician said, gesturing as if he could not get the words out fast enough, "recording is indiscriminate! Clanging jackhammer or golden throat, it picks up both with equal fidelity."

The conversation continued in a frenzy of technical jargon, and soon the counter was scattered with drawings, coffee cups and discarded pencil nubs. As my father haggled with the technician over the cost of the receiver and the time needed to construct it, I wandered to a corner dominated by a gleaming cherrywood cabinet containing a series of tiny drawers with tarnished silver handles. Some were open; when I tried to push one shut, it wouldn't budge. Slipping my hand inside, I scooped up a handful of cool round objects which shortly revealed themselves to be bits of exquisite scrimshaw. I stuck my hand in another drawer and withdrew a needle for a record player. Further exploration yielded other things: a bone hairpin, paper clips, and a few pieces of movable type—the letter L, a question mark, an ampersand. A final foray rewarded me with a marvelous telescope the size of my thumb.

The telescope struck me as so precious I couldn't imagine living without it, and so for the first time in my life, I sidled up to my father and dared ask him to buy it. My father took the telescope and rolled it in his palm, scowling slightly. How could a little girl know the value of such an object? Not that it was rare or expensive; such things could be found at any hobbyist's shop. But my father, I believe, imagined that my request indicated an undesirable development of my character, a troubling propensity for abstraction that I might have inherited from my mother—who was, at that moment, engaged in a closed-door debate with three tweedy, imposing men (her tenure committee) over the applicability of kinship analyses to the study of scientific research.

I SUPPOSE THE TELESCOPE fascinated me because I was learning astronomy. I had discovered that the seven stars of the Pleiades move from east to west across the winter sky, followed by Orion. I also learned that each star in the Pleiades represented one of the seven daughters of Atlas, who balanced the world on his broad shoulders, and I read that Orion, wearing his spangly triple-starred belt, made his yearly pilgrimage across the sky in order to woo the sisters, one after the other. Then, discarding my books for the empirical sky, I found to my disappointment that I could see only six of the seven stars clearly; the seventh was always just a faint blue haze on the periphery of my vision. What was she like, this mystery daughter of Atlas? I imagined a shy girl fitted out in somber clothes.

Father's study was a refuge for me in those days. He had a marvelous record collection and a machine that permitted him to mix all kinds of sounds together. One morning he made me a tape on which I heard: a train getting up speed, a chicken clucking, a blade on a whetstone, fanfares, hunting horns, the pop of a cork, gurgling of liquid decanted, a violin solo, and a few deep notes from a cello. "What story am I telling, Annalise?" I couldn't even begin to say. He continued, "If I were to play them backwards, I would say it was the sound of someone's biography, told in reverse, as if broadcast from a distant star."

In addition to radio, Father nurtured an interest in local history. It came as no surprise to anyone, therefore, that while we lived in New Bedford, Father should have re-discovered *Moby Dick* and devoted himself to the particulars of Melville's life. He told me the story of Melville's neighbor, a woman named Agatha Robertson who was a young wife when her husband, leaving New Bedford in search of work, vowed to send word as soon as he found a job. Though she waited seventeen years, the promised letter never arrived. "Imagine," Father urged me, "every day she'd walk to the postbox and find nothing from him. Nothing!" She waited so long, Father said, that the mailbox itself began to rot. Overwhelmed by Queen Anne's lace, the post collapsed, and a family of robins took up residence inside. "Seventeen years for a single letter!" Father paused, considering. "One could not expect such a thing from your mother."

I HAD FEW TOYS—Mother's itinerant career made accumulation of possessions impractical—but I did own a marvelous deck of natural history cards with letters on one side and pictures on the other. The letter A, for instance, concealed an ailanthus; P stood for a green parrot with pinhead eyes of cochineal; and M represented a tiny mollusk that Father identified as *Nucella lapillus*, found on the coasts of Britain and Ireland and used for making crimson dye "since the days of Pliny the Elder."

But even these could not compete with my body's new, unfamiliar demands. I didn't know what was happening to me. On one of our walks, Father bought me a conch which he held against my ear until I heard something rumble. At night in my bed, when pleasure burst beneath my small fingers, I cupped the shell to my chest and imagined my heartbeat etching itself over the shell's pale interior, ready for playback some day. And when one night I dreamed of a man beside me, my ears were suffused with the sound of old starlight, a distant bloodrush roar.

ONE SUMMER MORNING, after we visit the electronics shop to check on the progress of Father's receiver, we stop at the butcher's, where we take a ticket and stand in line before the gleaming meat cases. My father is so excited by the technician's progress that he can barely tolerate the wait, and so he fidgets, hopping up and down on the balls of his feet and whispering his plans for what he calls his "acoustic tasimeter" in my ear. I'm not listening, for my head is full of the rich smell of blood and whiffs of disinfectant that don't quite cover an odor of something rotten. The butchers smile and merrily wish my father good day while they bustle between the flayed carcasses stretching from meat-hooks, row upon row of red cuts larded with white fat. Another case contains a pile of pigs' heads, hairless and the singular pink of strawberry ice cream, each face a mask, expressive yet frozen. Someone calls my father by name. When he looks up, the butcher lifts one of these obscene faces by the ear and shouts, "*Ain't* she pretty? You could make some fine headcheese today!" Dark blood trickles thinly from a nostril. My father gasps and dashes from the shop.

I follow, only to find my father on the sidewalk, hunched over a pool of vomit and grasping for his handkerchief. I help him to stand and then to walk, his weight twitching heavily against me all the way home.

FATHER WAS ILL for two months. During that time, Mother came and went as usual, her orbit mysterious but regular. Father did not leave the house.

The first weeks of Father's confinement were terrifying. When he was not twisted damply in his sheets, his pallid face by turns hot and cold, he raged about the bedroom, his stomping plainly audible even in the basement, where I loaded soiled bedclothes into the washer. Upstairs, in his delirium, the ticking of his wristwatch maddened him, threatening to eclipse his own heartbeat. And although, while he slept, I removed the watch from his wrist and tucked it into my mother's jewelry box, he woke the next day raving, this time certain that he was being buried alive. He heard the mailman's steps to and from the letterbox as shovelsful of dirt on his coffin.

When at last the fever broke and Father felt well enough to return to his study, he asked me to help sort his accumulated correspondence. Before he fell ill, he had been working on a play called *Dead Stars Singing* and his research had led him into correspondence with a radio astronomer who lived across the continent, in Penticton, Canada, and whose work involved the detection of residue from supernovas, in the form of radio waves. Preparing his response to the astronomer's dispatches, Father equipped me with a fountain pen and dictated his replies. While I sat, pen at the ready, in a patch of sunlight on the floor, Father mused at his desk: "Imagine what those stars have to tell us! The most recent celestial death-rattle is so old it might contain an echo of the first human cry, the first gasp or gurgle upon emergence from the primordial swamp!"

Once begun, Father's recovery was swift and total. Soon it was time to return to the electronics shop, where the finished receiver awaited my father's inspection. On the appointed day, we arrived at the shop to find the carpet freshly vacuumed and the detritus of old electronics cleared away. The technician, wearing a clean tie for once, had set the new receiver on a pedestal draped with a fine cloth. The workmanship was marvelous: The receiver boasted knobs of turned walnut and a console fitted into a casing with details made from mother-of-pearl. The technician explained that he'd already had some success capturing signals from distant radio stations and he was eager to work with my father if further fine-tuning was necessary. Father signed a check with a flourish. The technician shook Father's hand, and then, gravely, he shook mine. On the counter, there was a fresh cup of tea for my father, who sipped it gratefully. I had been given a special treat: a piece of dark chocolate molded in the shape of a star. As I broke off a point and conveyed it to my mouth, my father turned to the technician and said, "That reminds me—is the tiny telescope still here?"

The technician shook his head. He'd sold it the week before. I must have looked crestfallen, for he lifted a finger and cried, *Wait!* Then he disappeared behind the curtain that led to the shop's back room.

Father could not keep his eyes off the receiver. After he finished his tea, he gathered the box up into his arms, as if testing its weight.

The technician reappeared carrying a large glass jar covered with a rag. In his other hand, he clutched what appeared to be a remote control. He placed the jar on the counter and inserted a wire into a small box attached to the jar; the wire's other end fitted into the remote. A second wire dangled down, with a plug attached. He stuck the plug into a wall socket and lifted the rag.

A monkey's head hung suspended in a lustrous, silver-flecked fluid. Its black hair drifted slowly, and then stood straight out as the technician cranked a knob on the remote. The head turned and its face came forward. The pink mouth opened and shut several times, and the eyelids twitched. "It's *aqua micans*," the technician said hurriedly, " an electrical medium, such that a current sent through it could cause the facial muscles to twitch—"

The monkey's mouth was filled with teeth. I could see rows of silver.

"The metal," the technician was saying, "transmits—"

He pushed more buttons, and the monkey's mouth moved faster. A high, keening noise modulated with something like speech, as if the monkey were speaking a language I knew but could not quite understand.

The monkey in *aqua micans* severely displeased my father. The receiver under one arm, he grabbed my hand and propelled me toward the door, snarling: "The child! For heaven's sake, *mind the child*!"

On the street, Father hailed a cab and, in the close dark of the back seat, he doubled himself over the receiver and clutched his head in his hands. When I touched his arm, he trembled, and his black eyes burned.

"That monkey should be pushing up daisies right now," he spat. "It doesn't belong in a display case."

When the cab pulled into our drive, Father murmured he felt unsteady. Would I please help him up the steps? I offered my arm and was astonished to feel, as with that horrible day at the butcher's, the bulk of his weight. As we made our way up, he held the receiver tightly under his free arm. Only when we reached the top did he let me go, in order to fish for his keys. But there was a light on inside. Mother was home. Why didn't he ring?

At last, he turned the key in the lock and as the door opened, I heard the rich, silty sound of my mother's singing:

Daisy, Daisy
Give me your answer do

Into the room danced my mother, nude but for a towel wrapped round her head, in the arms of a stranger. They circled, and then she saw us and stopped. Looking first at me and then at my father, she pulled the stranger to her chest. I was aware of my father's hand on my neck, squeezing me hard, harder. The receiver crashed to the floor, its inner mechanism sprung out in wild coils. My father gripped the back of my neck so tightly the pain rose through my throat and into my ears, and the last sound I heard was my mother's laughter.

Alberto: A Case History

ONE WET DAY IN EARLY SPRING, the doorbell rang while I was in the front hall folding an umbrella. I opened the door to find a boy slumped on the step. A grimy elbow poked through a hole in his sleeve, and a swag of dull yellow hair fell to his nose, which was tipped with a café-au-lait stain shaped like Australia. His mother, or someone, had pinned a note to his lapel: *Alberto has been taken by the devil.*

In those days, our asylum was located on the outskirts of Bad Dürrenmatt, a village distinguished by a three-arched stone bridge that crossed the Ähr outside the old town wall. The bridge was a source of local pride and, in the year of Alberto's arrival, the villagers of Bad Dürrenmatt had marked its bicentennial by shooting off fireworks until late in the night, in a ceremony that the local authorities intended for a double purpose: not only to commemorate the bridge, but also to substitute, symbolically, for the annual *coulinage*, during which the villagers gathered in the orchards to burn lichen from the filbert trees. Their fruit is a well-known local delicacy, but that year, the ritual had been forbidden. The villagers worried that without the annual rite of burning, the trees would succumb to the predations of caterpillars; and so the elders had called upon the vicar to perform an exorcism. But just as the vicar excommunicated the bugs in absentia with a flick of a finger dipped in consecrated wine, his son released a hedgehog into the congregation. The panicked animal found the magistrate directly and bit him on the toe. The magistrate flung the creature against the wall, where it expired, and then he chased the child into the river, where he was swept away. The police found his body a few days later, caught in the roots of a willow. After that, the villagers were seized by a mania that made demons out of all but the most docile of the village children, more than a few of whom were, it was whispered, stuffed into baskets and thrown into the river. But for every child who was supposedly killed, several others were merely abandoned on our doorstep, and we took them in, knowing they were not demons at all but simply children—ordinary, shivering, frightened children with nowhere else to go. On the mild day of his arrival, I assumed that Alberto was one of them, the forsaken children of Bad Dürrenmatt.

"Alberto," I said, shaking him. He stood slowly, then staggered into the kitchen, where he sank to the floor and closed his eyes with a small sigh that was at once so brave, and so innocent, I caught my breath. Though Alberto was dirty and possibly quite sick, anyone could see that he was a fine boy, about four years old, whose equanimity was such that, upon finding himself suddenly reliant upon the goodwill of strangers, he simply lay down in a warm corner and went to sleep, even while the cook and the housekeeper tut-tutted over him and my father, oblivious, shouted into the phone to the city councilman.

At that time, in addition to taking in unwanted children, my father and I were pioneering novel methods at the asylum, based on the old philosophy that the best way to treat the mind was by cultivating the body. Although the classical name for our approach, *mens sana in corpore sano* is simple to say, it is difficult to make therapeutic without extraordinary effort, and our treatments, necessarily unorthodox, had come to the attention of the local authorities, who felt that such individualized treatments did not square with the collectivity-minded politics of the time. In addition, we'd begun to get hints of disapproval from the state—pamphlets exhorting us to put our patients to work in fields and gardens, to encourage them to hold meetings, to distribute tasks and rewards, and otherwise organize themselves into a little society. The advice was, not surprisingly, wholly impractical. Most of our patients either didn't speak or babbled incomprehensibly. Those few who could follow simple directions more often than not took to their beds when asked to do anything at all. Nonetheless we read and filed these directives and, once a year, we received a visit from an inspector who shared a meal, took a look around, and then departed, whistling as he staggered down the drive carrying boxes of port and cigars—gifts from the grateful families of our patients. In this way, my father said, our success ensured our survival.

That year, however, our port and cigars had not worked so well and my father was under pressure to change his therapies or close up shop.

"Of course the sanatorium is necessary," he barked into the phone. Making his case to the councilman, my father went on to describe the habits of one of our more perplexing patients, Uwe Brandt, who had a penchant for keeping his nail clippings in a silk purse around his neck. Imagine: years of clippings folded into a pocket of blush-colored silk closed with a velvet drawstring. On the phone, my father described the clippings in detail, then asked, "What if he decided, one day, to clip something else?"

The councilman must have had to concede the point, for my father put his hand over the mouthpiece and shook with laughter.

I smiled back, but distractedly, for Alberto had again fallen asleep, this time having wedged himself between the kitchen table and the sink, and I was obliged to yank him free. My strain must have shown because my father's face grew serious.

He shook his head, as if to say *Another one?*, then returned to his call, where he pressed his advantage, conjuring the specter of Bad Dürrenmatt besieged by madmen wielding hair clippers and pruning shears, and informed the councilman we had *at least* one hundred sick souls in our care—a tremendous exaggeration. Yes, my father said, as if to an imbecile, they *can* be violent. Yes, he emphasized, in a paroxysm of coughing that set my teeth to grinding, even the women. *Especially* the women.

As their argument continued, I helped Alberto undress and directed him into a tub. It wasn't easy, for I had to keep rousing him. As I scrubbed him with a washcloth, dissolving grime from beneath his fingernails and between his toes, my father took a softer tone with the councilman, inviting him to see our facility for himself. My father described our courtyard, where we constructed a grotto filled with hot and cold pools that foamed in recesses ornamented with leaves and flowers, and where the wet air was charged with essences selected especially for each patient's complaint: lavender for melancholy, orange blossom for seizure, vanilla for loss of speech. When my father mentioned the fountains stocked with fat carp, Alberto's eyes flicked open. "Would you like to see our courtyard?" I asked. Alberto nodded. As I brushed the wet hair out of his eyes, I told him about how we had mixed old moss with buttermilk and then poured it between the flagstones where, a few days later, a lush green carpet bubbled up. In the middle of the courtyard, I continued, there was a circular bench faced with tiny tiles arranged in a mosaic my father had once seen in a photograph of the Alhambra.

Alberto asked where his mother was. As I had no answer, I poured a saucepan of warm water down his back. He slumped against me, wetting my shirt.

In the afternoon, as we sat in my office, Alberto perked up again when he noticed a carved lion on my desk. I'd picked it up at the village five-and-dime, a cramped little basement store owned by Frau Schnacker, an old widow of the cranky and unfortunate sort that thrive in small towns like ours. I liked the shop because the sheer quantity and variety of stuff crammed within it reminded me of the rich and exotic cities I kept telling myself I would someday visit, making them more than just names on a map: Cairo, Peshawar, Detroit. I was thinking particularly of Cairo when I handed the lion to Alberto who, after a moment's deliberation, twirled the carving around his index finger.

"He is Egyptian," I informed Alberto. At least that's what Frau Schnacker told me.

"H-h-he is alabaster," Alberto replied, his first words to me. A smile broke across his face like a fish surfacing in one of our courtyard ponds, glimmering for a second before returning to darkness. Perhaps he was not as sick as I thought. But although we sat in my office for another quarter hour, Alberto only sank back into the armchair and closed his eyes. Later, in my notebook, I reflected on our exchange: *Alberto is not well, but he is teaching me things already. Today he reminded me how easy it is to confuse origins with substance! It's as if he knows what I keep forgetting: These primitive things, they exist for us.*

MADNESS HAS BEEN my family's business for generations. When my grandfather died, my father inherited the sanatorium. He worked there for years, and I joined him after the university at Leipzig refused to grant me my medical diploma, citing bureaucratic reasons, despite my having completed all the requirements for the degree. Although there was plenty to do at the sanatorium and my father, who knew my abilities, was not about to refuse to let me work, I returned home unwillingly. Leipzig marked the limit of my horizons, and I longed to see the ocean and the great cities. But even if one did manage to make one's way, over pitted and often closed roads, all the while handing out ballpoint pens and cigarettes, to the airport, the political situation made travel abroad impossible. So I plied my trade at the sanatorium while my father haggled with the university over the issue of my diploma.

At the asylum, my father proved himself a natural diagnostician, for he was observant and he revered the telling, personal detail. Indeed, his favorite patients suffered not only from psychic maladies but also from other misfortunes that each stamped their illnesses with particularities that added an interesting dimension to the case, even when they were not, strictly speaking, pathological. So, for instance, we treated a man who, due to a farm accident, had a pipe stuck through his head. He was fine at all times except when he happened to hear a series of notes from "Toreador," which caused the pipe to vibrate and set off thoughts of murder— and the year he had his accident the whole of Europe was so mad for revivals of *Carmen* that the music poured out of windows and cars. Ice cream trucks even used the tune to summon children in the village. To treat him, my father had to abandon our usual, indirect methods and sought to relieve the patient by directly mechanical means: Using a torch, he burned off bits of the pipe and then, having strapped the patient to a gurney for safety, he played all of *Carmen* on the record player to test his new design.

For my part, I looked after the children: the ones who ripped whiskers off cats and legs off frogs, who wounded themselves and picked incessantly at the scabs, the children who refused to speak and those who would not stop speaking. The children's troubles were less particular than those of our adult patients, whose characters had been dented and creased, each differently, by time and experience. But what the children lacked in clinical fascination, they more than made up for in their capacity to heal. By the time Alberto arrived, I was also responsible for the children who, as a result of the mania that had gripped the town, had been abandoned on our front steps. My father and I agreed that taking them in was the right thing to do—as if we had a choice! By the time they'd found us, their parents had already inflicted upon them a wound that was certain to linger. Better to get them early, I told my father. They'd become our patients sooner or later anyway. Perhaps even more than the officially sick children, these unlucky bundles were our destiny.

ONE NIGHT AFTER I had tucked Alberto into bed, I joined my father for a walk along the Ähr. As we neared the old three-arched bridge, we parted the bushes and followed a narrow footpath to the riverbank, which was crowded with daffodils. My father went first, sucking on a corncob pipe. I trailed behind him, picking my way through the muddy grass and breathing plumes of cherry-vanilla smoke.

"What shall we do with Alberto? He's easily overstimulated."

"He stutters, too." I expounded briefly on the diseases indicated in children who stutter, in order to generate a differential diagnosis.

"But are you sure he is sick?"

Of course he was sick. My father could be so stubborn! I struggled not to break into the pleas of a girl wanting to keep a stray cat she'd found in the yard. *No.* Alberto's illness was plainly evident in the tilt of his head (timidity), and the way he leaned on me in the kitchen tub (exhaustion), and, of course, there was his stutter.

"Which could," I reminded my father, "mean anything."

As we paced the riverbank, I outlined a regimen based on our usual therapies. Alberto would first get as much rest, sunlight, air, and good simple food as possible. When he was no longer quite so thin and pale, we would start him on a course of therapy to bring him to life, as it were, from within—a purely sensory therapy, a therapy without words except when they could be put in the service of sensation.

"Elaborate," my father commanded, waving his pipe.

"I have read that when you're in a foreign country, you can sometimes forget the word for a common thing, say 'raspberry', in your *Muttersprache* while you still haven't learned the local word. And then, when you're in this frame of mind, neither here nor there, someone hands you a raspberry tart and the flavor is overwhelming and familiar and exotic, all at once. You cannot domesticate it immediately with words."

"So you have a kind of access, a rush of pure sensation—" My father lodged the pipe in a corner of his mouth, removed a pen and a small notebook from his pocket, and began to scribble.

"The word finally means something," I said. "Or, more precisely, you finally know what you mean."

We neared the foot of the bridge. I pointed out some nets that had been strung across the pediments of the arches.

"Oh, those." My father was unimpressed. "We're trying to save some children, I suppose. I hear the town council ruled on it."

"But they look so flimsy."

"Thus the poor," my father murmured, "are always with us." He re-lit his pipe. "All this theory is very interesting but what specific treatment do you propose for Alberto?"

"We'll aim for pure pleasure and plenty of contrast. He'll eat orange marmalade and green apples, run his hands through sand and over vellum, listen to Bach in the morning and Stravinsky after lunch. All with no distinctions, no history or context, and certainly no rules except that each experience should happen separately, so he is not overwhelmed. He will enjoy each new thing for itself."

"You will spoil him." My father often said the opposite of what he meant, and this was no exception. Through a cloud of smoke, he was beaming. I had done well.

I wiggled my toes, suddenly warm despite the cold. Maybe someday I would run the asylum myself.

"In learning what pleases him and what does not," my father said, "Alberto will be free to become who he is, without being burdened with having to learn about things that can mean nothing to him."

"Exactly," I said. "You can't learn how raspberries taste from a dictionary."

Later, as my father helped me write up our plan, a fit of coughing seized him. It lasted for several minutes, after which he choked up something into a handkerchief.

"Father—"

He waved me off. "It's nothing, Lunette."

ALTHOUGH MY FATHER'S COUGH worried me, the next day I felt strangely buoyant, as if my whole being were rising up, tingling, with the moist spring air and the smell of the earth that it carried. I bought a pound of black cherries from the grocer, then I stopped at Frau Schnacker's and felt, for once, no irritation when I had to ring five times before the proprietress came to the door in her housedress.

"Something's different about you," she said, standing in the doorway regarding me with her one good eye. (The other one was glass and did not move, ever.) "I know! You have a new boyfriend."

"I don't think so," I replied, slipping past her. Inside, the shop was gloomy, and I made a beeline for the dry goods section, where Frau Schnacker padded up behind me as I was fingering the spice chest. I opened a drawer and leaned in to sniff: black cherries.

"What's this?"

"Mahlab, from the Levant. It's made from cherry pits. They use it for baking." Frau Schnacker rubbed her bad eye, which squeaked.

"I'll take an ounce," I said. She measured the powder for me, then packed it into a vial, which she stoppered with a cork. The vial fit snugly in the palm of my hand.

As she handed me my change, she said, "Are you sure you don't have a boyfriend? I always say, you know, all work and no play makes a girl"—here she paused—"rather strange."

Frau Schnacker knew very well I did not have time for boyfriends. When she talked like this, it was just to twit me. Her real problem was, she didn't like the sanatorium and she kept pushing the council to close it. If I got married and left, she would have less trouble convincing my father to leave also—or so I imagined.

As I left I caught Frau Schnacker out of the corner of my eye as she pulled up her skirt, gathered it at her crotch, and, grinning lewdly, shook it with both hands. Peeved, I let the door slam behind me. How curious that one rudeness should follow another like this, each one the cause of the next. I crossed a narrow side street, the vial like a hot ingot in my pocket, and scrambled over the old town wall, where I thought I caught a glimpse of Uwe Brandt in a sunlit stand of birch trees. Maybe it wasn't Uwe. But someone was there, for I heard him laugh.

Later, I uncorked the vial and put a pinch of mahlab on my tongue. It tasted exactly like the moment when, after you eat a black cherry, you spit out the pit. This, I decided, is where I would start with Alberto—with a bowl of black cherries and, after that, a bit of mahlab on a spoon.

ALBERTO ENDURED my lessons solemnly, showing the patience of a boy twice his age. At my urging, he chewed fennel leaves, rounds of salt licorice, and the special mahlab; he played with prisms and collected stones from the garden; he listened to symphonies and bebop, and to renditions of *Für Elise* that I played on the old pianoforte below the stairs. To avoid precipitating him into slumber, I limited the duration of our sessions and chose my words with care: Taste a bit of this, Alberto, if it won't be too much for you; look at that, if you please; and what do you think, my dear Alberto, about this other thing? Sometimes he accompanied me and my father on our rounds; he seemed to enjoy the other patients, especially a quiet woman who suffered from insomnia, to whom he gave his extra licorice. To my disappointment, however, Alberto had said almost nothing since our interview in my office, although he clearly enjoyed eating black cherries and playing with the alabaster lion, which he arranged on the windowsill in various poses, along with some toy soldiers I picked up for him at Frau Schnacker's.

Then, one day, we had a breakthrough. I was upstairs with a girl who was prattling about the King of Siam, every so often stopping to ask if she was "being wearisome," and otherwise behaving in such a way that I could not help feeling as tired as she apparently feared to make me. Worse, upon noticing my exhaustion, she had instituted compulsory rest breaks, which bored me even more. We were in the middle of one of these when a shriek rose up from the kitchen.

What had happened was this: Evidently, Alberto had been poking around the pantry when he found the six buckets of filbert paste that my father and I had received as gifts from a patient from a family of chocolatiers. We hadn't been sure quite what to do with the gift. Although neither of us liked sweets, filbert paste was a delicacy for which we knew we could get a tidy sum on the black market. But our plan, like all plans, required time to execute, time that we just didn't have. While we dithered, Alberto found the buckets and slotted them into a plan of his own. When the cook wasn't looking, he'd sneaked into the pantry and, with a butter knife, pried the top off one of them, and then another, and another. And now Alberto was prancing around naked, slathered head-to-toe in filbert paste and, furthermore, eating it straight from the buckets in huge mouthfuls with a wooden spoon.

His smile, when he saw me, was bright white and wicked. My heart skipped a beat, and some mania seized me: I plunged both my hands up to the shoulders into the nearest bucket. Alberto whooped and waved his spoon. "Eat it! Eat! Eat!"

I took one mouthful, then another, and soon we were both gobbling filbert paste while the cook clucked and shook her head. All the while, I was thinking: *At last, it has happened. I have been here too long and now I am out of my mind.* But my thoughts seemed to have no connection to my actions. Indeed, I felt cleaved in two. The rational, thinking half of me could only watch as we overturned the buckets and slipped on the tiles, sliding across the sweet pools until we were both brown and sticky, and all the filbert paste was either smeared on the floor or eaten up. Then we rested, spent, beneath the window like two frosted gingerbread people. The cook, offended, left in a huff, shouting: "There is no WAY I will cook another thing in that filthy kitchen, for you filthy swine, wallowing filthily in your own filthy FILTH!" And so we had no choice but to clean up the mess ourselves, as best we could, when we finally returned to our senses, or they to us.

We agreed not to tell my father. I made Alberto shake my hand to seal the promise, then I wondered whether, in doing so, I had just breached a principle of Alberto's therapy. After all, promises are made and kept or broken in time, and time is the enemy of sensation. I decided to note the development in my journal and see what happened.

Later that night, some villagers, tipped off no doubt by the cook and armed with mops and brooms, punched through our front door and swarmed into the kitchen. Thinking fast, I pulled Alberto behind the door, where we watched in horror as the intruders took broomsticks and bats to our oven and pantry. I thought I saw Frau Schnacker in the chaos, but the villagers were wearing hoods that rendered them indistinguishable. We gathered from their bursts of shouting that they intended to scrub the place until it shone and then beat us with their cleaning implements until we had, as one of them snarled through her balaclava, the devil driven out of us. My father, who had descended the stairs to see what the fuss was about, called out for peace and order while Alberto and I emerged from our hiding place and drove the ladies off with brooms of our own. Afterward, my father retired to his room without a word and I heard him coughing late in the night. His illness had gotten so severe he coughed in his sleep, without waking up. He woke me up instead, and I listened, and worried about him.

Not long after the filbert-paste incident, my father stopped eating. He said only his pipe gave him pleasure and grimly overrode my claim that the pipe smoke was killing him. I didn't press the issue. It was clear to me that he had decided to die, and since the decision was made, we did not talk any more about it. There was after all nothing much left to discuss; to die was only what he wanted, and what you want, as he always said, is what you are. With his decision, my dreams of travel receded. There was too much to do, and no time for dreaming. When my father took to his bed for good, I began to find new homes for our patients. They left us one by one. But I could not discard Alberto.

One night, my father died. I held his hand as the life flowed from it, his pulse fading as the sun rose. With help from Alberto, who was quiet and stoic, I washed my father's body, wrapped him in a fresh sheet, and had him buried at the edge of our woods. On the same day, the last of our patients left for another sanatorium. After that, Alberto and I spent most of our time together in the kitchen, where we were distracted by the company of our new cook, a lively girl of about fourteen who doted on Alberto nearly as much as I did.

In the meantime, ever more threatening letters arrived every day: the government wanted to take our property. It belonged to the people. And so on.

I ignored these letters, just as I ignored the titters and whispers that followed me as I went among the townspeople. I told myself the rumors were just part of being in the asylum business: someone always wants to run you and your patients out of town. In any event it was not hard to find other things to focus on. Alberto was speaking more and gaining weight; his stutter had diminished; and his education absorbed us both. When we graduated from taste and smell to touch, I brought him books whose leaves were made of fabric, gifts from an upholstery salesman whose hysterical wife had stayed with us for a time. The samples ranged from simple canvas to densely woven paisleys, plaids, and even a deep blue velvet. Alberto traced letters in the fabric and cut them out, a leaf at a time. Then he pasted the fabric letters onto his wooden ones and placed each, one after the other, in his mouth.

Once I asked him to spell out whatever he was feeling. The word he chose was: ABFALL. Trash. Spelled out in fragments of houndstooth silk, a tender pink dimity, organza, madras, an Eton stripe.

I chided him: "The combination is nonsensical, Alberto."
He shrugged.

The next afternoon, I asked him what it felt like to speak freely, without his stutter. In response he pitted a bowl of black cherries and stacked the pits in the shape of a rude pyramid. When he finished, he crammed the pitted cherries into his mouth. The juice ran down his chin in a thin red line which he swept back into his mouth with a finger, the gesture fierce, fast and sure. When the bowl was empty, he smiled. His teeth were dark red.

ALTHOUGH ALBERTO HAD once slept too much, he now began to wake during the night and, even as he tried, could not lull himself back to sleep. Worried, I assigned him a new room, away from the kitchen's racket. I set a mattress with some blankets on the floor—and nothing else. Nothing. That was the rule. There was a window that he could open if he liked, over which I'd hung a curtain. Despite my precautions, on the first night when darkness arrived even this simple room was too distracting, and Alberto required hours to settle down to sleep.

There was no help for it. We would have to repaint.

The following day we went to town for supplies. On the way home, we passed Frau Schnacker's. In the window, a wooden rabbit dressed as a soldier caught Alberto's eye. He stood looking at it, transfixed. "Let's go in," I suggested, setting our parcels on the pavement and trying the door, which was locked as usual. As I rang the bell, Alberto began to fidget, a behavior that was unusual for him which I put down to excitement. After a moment, Frau Schnacker appeared in her usual grimy housedress and regarded us balefully from behind the glass. Then she heaved open the front door and Alberto bounded in. I followed with the paint and brushes, which I tucked into a corner near the door, beside the chipped porcelain umbrella stand.

"You break it, you own it," she warned. And then, in a whisper just loud enough for me to hear, "A wild boy will need beating, *jawohl*."

A moment later, a meowing cat scurried over my feet and clambered up a curtain, which tore just at the moment that Alberto, turning to see what had made such a strange noise, upset a pyramid of turnips with his elbow. Frau Schnacker hollered, rattling teacups in the china chest. Frightened, Alberto grabbed a bundle of radishes from a bin and chewed on them, taking frantic bites. Bits of radish spewed everywhere. Incensed, Frau Schnacker chased him around the shop, brandishing her broom. "Foolishness! Foolishness!"

She cornered Alberto by the paperback display. I stumbled over a pile of plastic fire engines and grabbed her broom just as she lifted it over her head to strike him. As Alberto cowered, his shirt pocked with radish, she and I grappled. She was so close I could smell how sour she was. Feeling me gain the advantage, she relinquished the broom and slipped into the recesses of the shop, where she croaked: "Why have you made this wicked boy?"

We made our way to the shop's front door. As I grabbed our cans of paint, the umbrella stand toppled and shattered. I could have sworn I felt Frau Schnacker's breath hot on the back of my neck. Holding Alberto's wrist tightly with my free hand, I dragged us both into the sunshine.

"You must beat him," Frau Schnacker snarled as the door slammed shut behind us, "to drive out the foolishness."

TOGETHER WE PAINTED THE ROOM—walls, floor, ceiling, moldings, everything—in coats of midnight blue, the paint so thick it dried on everything like a rubbery skin. After we finished, we shuttered the window and extinguished the lights. The room thrust us deep and untethered into the vault of the night. There was no up or down, no here or there. "We are astronauts," I said, imagining satellites chattering along the ecliptic. Dizzied, I tumbled onto a mattress and begged Alberto to open the curtain, otherwise I was going to fall asleep. His answer was a snore.

Nights in the blue room, I curled around him as he slept. Sometimes, when there was a moon, I took a chance that Alberto might wake and drew back the curtain to let the light filter over us. In the dappled dark, Alberto smelled sweet-salty, like haystacks, cut clover, and what I imagined was the sea.

ONE DAY I RETURNED from the market to find the place wrecked—in the courtyard, the fountains and tubs were smashed and the walls of the conversation pit were covered with obscenities, many of them having to do with cleanliness and purification. Someone had taken a hatchet to the piano and all our books smoldered in a pile. In the corner, a broom leaned against the wall and beside it, like an offering, there was a pile of excrement. And the *silence*—so thorough was this demonic purge, even the sparrows had been murdered, one by one, each lying on the ground with its neck twisted. Though much was destroyed, it took only a moment to catalogue what was missing: Alberto. And the alabaster lion on my desk.

At the market the next day, when I asked some women washing towels at the fountain if they knew who destroyed our asylum, they turned their backs and wrung out their rags as if I weren't there. When I approached Frau Schnacker's shop, I heard hurrying footsteps and then the sound of the bolt in the lock. I banged at the window. Frau Schnacker appeared, glaring, and snapped the blinds shut. The councilman would not return my calls. I searched for Alberto, stalking up and down the old fortification wall, and then along the banks of the Ähr, all the way to the bridge and back. One night, I woke to the smell of burning flesh, and I knew I could not stay any longer; frightened, I left Bad Dürrenmatt the following day for Berlin where I rented a room near the train station and sat by the window, watching passengers get on and off. After a time, a letter arrived: I could either return to the asylum and convert it to some practical use, or I could let the council of Bad Dürrenmatt do the same and lose the property forever. As much as the council wanted the property for its own use, it did not want the trouble of administering it. If I came back, I would act as its manager. Curiously, when I called the councilman to say I was frightened of what the villagers might do if I returned, he assured me that I would be perfectly safe at my old residence, and that I need fear nothing from the people of Bad Dürrenmatt, who were just happy that the lunatics and the possessed children were gone.

It saddened me to return, but since I had neither a diploma nor references, I did not have any prospects anywhere. So I went back to our asylum, where I converted our rooms—the dormitories and the precious therapeutic tubs, the dispensary, the cafeteria—into office space that I rented to podiatrists, dermatologists, and others who treat diseases you can see and touch, diseases of the exterior. I thought of Alberto constantly; the fantasy I liked best was that he was living happily on his own somewhere, making his own way while keeping the alabaster lion close. At night, however, this pleasant illusion receded and my mind filled with terrible visions of Alberto bruised and broken, his yellow hair matted with blood. In truth, I was the one who felt forsaken. I knew that, by imagining him like this, I could take a kind of revenge; and I could punish myself for letting the villagers destroy us, and for letting him get away. My father would have said I was having it both ways, being angry at Alberto and angry at myself. In the end, I suppose, I was just angry. Helpless and angry.

In time, the visions faded, as they do. I slept, for comfort, in Alberto's blue room, and I kept an office under the eaves in the attic where I found enough peace to write his case history. I published it, to some acclaim, and as a result I finally traveled. Our work—for it is as much Alberto's as it is mine—brought me to the very cities I had longed to see, and many others besides. I even visited the Alhambra in Grenada, where I looked but failed to find the mosaic that inspired my father's design for our garden conversation pit. I made each new city my own in small ways, by taking photos until I could not look another moment into the viewfinder, writing to fill ten journals and then ten more. In a year, I moved around so much that I was home only three sad days in early spring, the time of daffodils. Reminders of Alberto cropped up everywhere. One day, while walking the footpath along the Ähr, I discovered the alabaster lion's face carved into the trunk of a birch tree. I found a pyramid of cherry pits on a bench in Paris. In San Francisco, I stumbled into Chinatown, where a man in an indigo kimono caught my eye. He turned away and dropped the robe, and the lion's face appeared again, tattooed across his back. In Tokyo, where I received an honorary degree, I was fêted with cherry blossoms. Everywhere I went, mothers of formerly silent, sleepy children who had benefited from the techniques I used with Alberto brought me branches bursting with the pink and white flowers; in a ceremony at the hotel they poured the blossoms over me from porcelain buckets; and one morning for breakfast a woman offered me a delicately scented tea made from the petals.

Psoriasis Memoir

I HAVE BEEN INVITED TO A PARTY. I have psoriasis. Have you noticed how it is possible to use the same word, "have," to say such different things? At any rate I have an obligation to appear somewhere appropriately dressed, which is not easy for someone in my condition. Most of the time, thanks to my psoriasis, my fondest desire is to scrape off my skin with my fingernails; clothing just gets between me and my itch.

The party is in honor of my doctor and friend, Barbara, who is treating my psoriasis. She is seven months pregnant. The party is being given by our mutual friend, Eric, who explained to me that the purpose of the party was to show support for Barbara by buying presents for the baby. Evidently, when one has a baby, it is customary to throw a party in order to be sure the baby begins with all the right accoutrements, as these things are important starting out. Not that I would know, never having had a child.

Because I so much prefer solitude, I live by myself in a small apartment of the type known as a "garden-level," which is a nice way of saying it is almost, but not quite, a basement. It does include a tiny garden full of the landlady's zinnias.

I don't have much contact with the landlady. I see her when she collects the rent, and every now and then we bump into each other on trash day. Our eyes meet, and then we lower them, exchange hellos, and push our trash into bins that have been set up for the purpose and chained to the fence so no one can steal them. I once used white plastic bags for my trash but I switched to black ones after accidentally meeting the landlady in this manner. The whole affair was very embarrassing because white bags are practically transparent. Thanks to this chance meeting I now understand how shameful it is to let someone else see everything I throw away.

The garden has become interesting to me because a few months ago a man who is no longer my lover gave me a packet of giant pumpkin seeds. Although my first impulse was to roast them, I decided against it since these were giant pumpkin seeds, and who knew what genetic modifications might occur, were I to ingest them, even in roasted form? I envisioned enormous hair follicles, fingernails like claws, skin cells the size of dinner plates. Having scared myself out of eating them, I planted the seeds in the garden while the landlady was away. A few sprouts emerged, but only one bona fide plant. I cared for it all summer and although I fully expected it to die, the pumpkin has only grown larger and larger. Soon I will have to decide what to do about it. I've seen pumpkins as big as Volkswagens and there isn't even room for a barbecue grill in the garden. Ironically, my thumb is not particularly green. In fact, at this moment it is reddish, slightly swollen, and itchy.

My thumb is important because I need my hands to write, and writing is how I make my living. My writing is not what you think of when you hear someone say, "I'm a writer." I don't make up stories; I don't have what's called a beat. Mostly I write summaries of market research; I also produce a monthly newsletter analyzing related trends. With so much pressing work to do, I was very concerned when, several weeks ago, the skin on my fingers began to burn and shortly thereafter to itch and to flake. I slathered my hands with cold cream and tried to pretend it wasn't happening. When the itch didn't go away, I made an appointment with the doctor recommended by Eric, the friend I've already mentioned, who owes me an article for my newsletter.

I would not mention Eric's debt, except that the reason he won't give it to me concerns his wife, Susan, who dislikes me. I am sure Eric would have ignored her wish that he not give me articles, but the situation is complicated. Eric is in debt, real debt and not just for articles, for a substantial sum, which Susan has promised to pay so long as Eric curtails his friendship with me. Although I don't know what this restriction entails, I am counting on Eric for this article. As a gesture of my good faith, I have declined to call Eric and nag him about the missing work, but to call it "a gesture of good faith" is not quite right either; since no one knows about this gesture except me, it is difficult to say whether it is truly effective, or if efficacy is even the correct way to evaluate it.

IF I SEEM CONFUSED, it may be on account of my psoriasis. According to my first doctor, the specialist I consulted before Barbara, confused thinking is sometimes a symptom of psoriasis. When she told me this, I asked whether the causal arrows might just as well point the other way, that is, whether psoriasis might actually be a symptom of confused thinking, because what could be more confused than the notion, evidently espoused by my own body, that bits and pieces of it, hitherto part of a smoothly functioning whole, were now suspect and to be cast out? What about the necessity of a periodic molt? The doctor smiled and said perhaps I would not produce such circuitous argumentation if I did not have psoriasis. While her remark made me angry, I did not fight back. I might have said, for instance, that I have been arguing in circles all my life so psoriasis probably has nothing to do with it.

Barbara, the doctor treating me now, was recommended by the first, who couldn't treat me because of a conflict of interest. Although she would not tell me this directly, I asked around after she stopped taking my calls. In the course of my research I learned that she is not only treating Eric, who as I said is married to Susan, but also the ex-lover Susan and I share: Darren. I found this curious. Something about the business-like way she snapped her surgical gloves into the bin marked **BIOHAZARD** suggested that she too was sleeping with Darren, and intended her efficiency as a rebuke, as if to let me know that she knew that what Darren hates most is inefficiency in a woman. Which, in retrospect, was probably true.

I have lately begun to wonder why everyone who has recently come into contact with me or with Darren is now seeing this doctor. Might we all have psoriasis? What an odd thought. Although the medical evidence says that the disease is non-contagious, this may be expert shorthand for saying that its transmission vectors are unknown. Or maybe it is just my mind that boggles, as a result of the confused thinking that I'm told is a symptom of psoriasis.

However, the possibility that we're all infected is not so farfetched, since everyone I know behaves in circular and confusing ways. For instance, there is a little story I like to tell about Darren. When he first moved to New York, he slept on a futon in his bedroom. The futon had traveled with Darren from his place in New Haven, where he and Susan had met. Darren later gave the futon to Barbara when she was evicted from her apartment in Brooklyn. Shortly after her eviction, Barbara and Darren became lovers. ("She seduced me," he said.) When Eric later moved into a spare room in Barbara's post-Brooklyn place, Barbara bought a new bed and gave the futon to Eric. By that time, Barbara and Darren had stopped sleeping together, but Eric had started seeing Susan. And now, as Brooklyn's peculiar, glassy morning light comes in through the window and settles on my itching hands, I wonder: What had it been like, to get the bed back but not the lover?

THE LAST TIME I SAW Barbara about my hands, she mentioned that psoriasis runs in families. The disease correlates with a recessive trait, which means it traveled on my genome along with my other recessive traits: my green eyes, my left-handedness, my AB blood type. The way these things ride the chromosomal smear reminds me of the old-time hobos hitching rides on freight trains during the Depression. The metaphor is not inappropriate; my great-grandfather, who treated his psoriasis with coal tar, hopped boxcars in and out of Kansas City in the 1930s. Through these traits my ancestors persist, itching and burning and ambitious to shed skin, like snakes.

A general reptilian quality runs in my family, too, and I suspect it may be related to psoriasis. For instance, my blood is thick and slow-running, and my blood pressure is so low I pass out when I stand too quickly. My father is the same way. Extreme hot or cold weather does not bother him, and he, too, is prone to passing out from low blood pressure. Although my father does not have psoriasis, he must have carried the recessive trait, because he did inherit the blood type. Yet he has brown eyes and is right-handed. Maybe there is some second-order genetic determinant, so that every left-handed green-eyed person in my family will develop a full-blown case of psoriasis, instead of being merely passive carriers. But that cannot be true, either, for my uncle is a green-eyed southpaw, and he is just fine. Maybe the truth is we're all waiting for triggers. Maybe we're all dermatological powder kegs, and I just happened to find the spark.

Incidentally, I have lately found myself unable to stop thinking about a story that I read in one of the magazines in Barbara's waiting room. The story is by a young writer, almost entirely unknown, whose talent is considerable. However, in his story he had referred to *The Brother's Karamazov*. At first I thought the possessive apostrophe was a joke but after thinking it over, I have become certain it is not a joke, merely a mistake. On my last visit to Barbara's office, I arrived early, located the story in the magazine, and blacked out the offending punctuation with a pen. Afterward, I couldn't stop thinking about the mistake—I mean, the joke—which, thanks to mass printing and distribution, had been repeated far and wide. My little surgery fixed the problem only once, and yet I had such faith in it, a tiny nip-and-tuck in the sagging world.

SOMEONE HAS SENT ME a packet of onions. I found them on the stoop today when I returned from Barbara's office. At first I thought perhaps the landlady had forgotten them—her door was open when I took them from the steps—but upon further reflection I think they must be a gift from Darren. No one else would leave a gift of onions on the steps for no reason, without a tag or a card.

But this gift from Darren, if indeed it is a gift, and if indeed it is from Darren and not from someone else, only poses further problems. Is Darren thinking of my pumpkin, and if so, does he expect a jack-o-lantern in return? A pumpkin pie? I will have to devote more thought to the matter, for it is obviously important to return the gift in sentiment if not in kind, and although I somewhat resent the imposition, devoting a few minutes each day to the question of appropriate reciprocation will be good for me. It will focus my mind and perhaps relieve the itch.

Now that I think of it, pumpkin comestibles might be a good idea, as the pumpkin is getting bigger and I am not sure what else to do. Sometimes a pumpkin will get too big and for this reason require a strict regimen of turning and shifting, lest it form a fatal patch of rot on the bottom, like a bedsore. Although I do not wish bedsores on my pumpkin, to which I now feel a strange attachment, observing such a regimen nonetheless seems extravagant labor for what is basically a glorified squash. These distinctions may seem picayune—what a word! I have just rediscovered it and have been occupied all morning with trying to find a discreet way to insert it into one of the articles in my newsletter—but I understand from the newspaper that they are vitally important to pumpkin farmers. For instance, if a pumpkin is more than thirty-five percent green, it is technically a squash and therefore cannot be entered in local contests where prizes are given for the largest and for the prettiest pumpkins, although—I am told—never for both at once.

THE ONIONS ARE OF THE TYPE known as "pearl": white, perfectly round, and so lovely I have decided to make a frittata out of them, to bring to Barbara's party. As I slice the onions into a pan of melted butter, it occurs to me that I have learned a great deal about cooking since I stopped seeing Darren.

When we were together, I made simple meals: omelets, macaroni and cheese, coffee and toast. Many of these were breakfasts, since Darren usually stayed the night. Out of politeness, I suppose. It was certainly not my cooking.

For instance, when I made Autocrat coffee for Darren, he complained that it was weak and blamed the coffee itself, not the coffee maker, which had been my hypothesis. As a result, I never bought Autocrat coffee again, and for good measure I also exchanged my old coffeemaker for a new Braun with cup-interrupt and many other functions intended to ensure the most flavorful brew and so on.

I haven't been able to bring myself to throw the Autocrat coffee away, however, so it sits in the back of the freezer along with the boxes of Velveeta cheese and the jars of minestrone and the bags of granola, also relics from my time with Darren. The minestrone was homemade, for Darren, but suffered from an overabundance of bay leaf. The granola was also homemade, and also for Darren, but I left it in the oven too long and it burned. When I was seeing Darren, I put the Velveeta in omelets, which were speckled with black on the outside and runny within, and I would serve them on what I hoped were cheerful yellow plates. I did not have a dishwasher at the time, and Darren would sometimes run a finger under his plate and wipe whatever he found there on a napkin. When Darren complained about "the government cheese," I corrected him. "It's Velveeta," I said. "I paid for it."

Although I would not presume to speak for anyone, I feel I can safely say these things for Darren: He was not fond of Velveeta. He did not like Autocrat or runny eggs. He probably wished I had a dishwasher. He once sterilized the toothbrush cup in the bathroom, saying, "I don't mind leaving a toothbrush, but I don't want to get a disease."

REFLECTING ON EVERYTHING that has happened since Darren left, I have come to some conclusions about personal relationships. Above all, I now believe that, in order for love to come into the world, one person must say to another: "I know you," and the other must believe it. At the precise moment when a person compels this belief of being known, of being understood, from another, there is love. Precision and timing are very important in this matter, as they are in cooking. Hygiene probably matters as well, though perhaps not as much as it did to Darren.

The problem with Darren was not that he compelled this belief from me, but *what* he made me believe. At such moments he did not merely say, "I know you," but he was very clear about *what* he knew. For instance, the morning after I met Susan for the first time at a party, he said, "Do you realize how your voice changes when you're with other people?" After I botched a presentation to my publisher, Darren remarked, "Do you ever notice how your hands shake when you're nervous?" And although I forget exactly when Darren discovered that my income doesn't normally permit me to spend a lot of money on what I wear, one afternoon he surprised me at a lunch counter when he leaned over my shoulder and whispered, "I know how much you paid for those shoes." Obviously, it is hard to be angry with a man who taught me so much about myself. My point is just that Darren was always precise, and his timing was often alarming.

This week, just before I discovered the onions on the doorstep, I splurged on expensive booties for the baby, so it won't have to worry about its footwear first thing out of the womb.

SINCE DEVELOPING PSORIASIS, I have learned many things about my condition. For instance: the word, "psoriasis," comes from the Greek word for "itch."

In the 1940s, a physician wrote that psoriasis is "a capricious disease that refuses to part with its innermost secrets."

When you have psoriasis, your skin acts endangered, producing new cells before the top layers have a chance to slough off, resulting in piles of backed-up flesh, silvery lesions indicating massive enforced obsolescence on a cellular level.

There is no cure for psoriasis. But of course, that is true of so many things.

In order to develop, psoriasis requires a trigger, which could be stress, an infection, or a wound. My grandfather developed psoriasis after he burned his hands opening a door that was on fire. Someone was trapped on the other side. My trigger may have been an infection, or it may have been the stress of completing a large project, or it may have been all the hot cups of coffee I have been holding while I sit at my computer experimenting with different ways to order the articles in my newsletter.

Lately I have dreamed that I will die like Ingeborg Bachmann, the Austrian poet, consumed by flames in my bed. I often wake from this dream with a random phrase running through my mind. Last night it was: itchy trigger finger.

But, these considerations aside, I think the trigger might be just what Barbara said at my consultation last week: "You let things get under your skin."

AT THE BABY SHOWER, as I add my jacket to the pile on Barbara's bed, Eric presses an envelope into my hands. "That article," he mutters, darting his eyes about the room. For a moment, my itch recedes; I consider ambushing him, having a quick furious fuck beneath the coats. My thought is so loud, he scuttles from the room.

A few minutes later, I find him in the kitchen with his arm wrapped tightly around Susan, who shakes her streaked pageboy to one side and fixes me with a look so baleful I can only shrug and wave Eric's envelope in what I hope is an apologetic way. *Men!* I want to say to her. *What can you do?* But the crowd comes between me and my good intentions. Other guests are in the kitchen too, including Darren, who refuses to catch my eye. The itch returns, a hot flare in my palms that creeps toward my elbows. Barbara passes me a wonderfully cool bowl of tiny carrots. I take one and offer the bowl to Darren. He smells faintly antiseptic, or perhaps I imagine this.

He stares at my hands, my face. I smile, and his gaze settles on the spot between my eyebrows. "What the hell happened to you?"

If I'm making him uncomfortable, I don't mind. Making him uncomfortable was all I ever did with him anyway.

Everyone has an opinion about my psoriasis. One earnest young guest, a medical student, offers a list of cures, ticking them off on his fingers in order of efficacy. When he finishes, I reply that I've heard of them all, and I remind him that there is no cure for psoriasis. There are, I say, only more or less effective treatments. Someone else suggests colloidal silver, which is notorious for turning the skin gray. I remark that I have seen people who take colloidal silver and they are the color of old nickels. You look at them, and they look back as if they already know what you are looking at. And, of course, they do.

Susan excuses herself. Eric follows her out.

For a while, I stand with Darren and Barbara by the butcher block. I tell stories about the pumpkin, fantasies of what might happen if it keeps growing at its present rate. Darren is astonished to hear anything grew at all. Barbara laughs and pats her stomach in the way she's adopted since she got pregnant. Will she keep the mannerism after the baby comes, or will she discard it with the placenta, out of deference to the main event? When she sweeps a pile of olive pits into the trash, I notice that the can is lined with white plastic and I think, what a welcome deprivation, to have nothing to be ashamed of.

Curiously, although the frittata is popular, no one mentions the onions. Perhaps they were not a gift from Darren after all, but from someone else. I make a mental note to look into it after the party ends.

Later, when Barbara opens my gift for the baby, Darren says, "Seven league boots."

"They are Manolo Blahniks," I say, which is the truth, although I am referring to my own shoes at the time.

Eleven, the Spelunker

DEAR —
You will be pleased, I think, to hear how I am getting on. The facilities are lovely. From my room, I have a clear view of the campus and the river, all the way to the corner where the glossy cube of our departmental building squats, visited at intervals by the shuttle bus, rocking on its shock absorbers, and by faculty members in station wagons that wait, directional lights blinking, at the intersection before tootling into the parking lot. From here, of course, our department is only a distant and amusing memory that only grows more amusing the more distant it becomes.

You might be interested to learn that one of the first people I met after arriving was—your mother! I found her in the lounge staring gloomily at the pay telephone through her greasy hair. She said she was trying to remember your number, which I was pleased to provide. In return, she gave me news of your adventures, foreign and domestic. She did not omit, moreover, an exhaustive review of the many successes you've had since you left our doctoral program—the one subject about which your otherwise loquacious mother refused to speak, as if the memory of your experiences, as you reported them to her, made me unworthy of further contact with you.

I do recognize the error of my ways, and I hope you will permit me to make amends by offering up a modest vignette that you might find useful for your literary pursuits. In doing so, I'm reminded of the class you took with me during your first semester. I'm thinking in particular of the events that, in the end, you turned to such triumphant and delicious effect in your novel, which your mother informed me has been translated into fifteen languages (and counting!), including Icelandic and even Russian, which translation, evidently, you supervised yourself.

Well, congrats, as they say. As I know from hard personal experience, such translations are easier said than done (although to be perfectly precise these things are not "said" at all). Now, if I may be permitted another small comment on a matter so large as *art*, I only wish that, in casting me as the pedantic, spinsterish anti-heroine in your book, you'd given me a fuller head of hair; baldness in women is so difficult, so tragic, that I think you, as a writer, might have misstepped in failing to imagine my character's suffering sufficiently. But, no matter—the book was hilarious and at one of our Friday seminars everyone in our department concluded that your *fame* was indeed well-deserved after we'd read and exhaustively discussed it, the book I mean, from the first sentence to the copy accompanying your author photo. Do you remember our Friday seminars? Those evenings in the big conference hall with the tiny smoked-glass observation room at the top and the wall of fogged Plexiglas overlooking the river? Even though you'd already left by the time we got around to discussing your novel, I kept expecting you to saunter in at any time, or jog past the windows while lifting a breezy, if not entirely respectful, hand to us as we suffered each other's company in the close room like restive ants in a too-small terrarium, just as you did, as a student, whenever the week's special lecture was not to your liking.

My little vignette concerns our newest tenured faculty member, the young Russian spelunker. I'm sure you remember him. What a revelation I have for you. Steel yourself, for here is the plain truth: He was a fake! A con artist! A joker! While it is true that, now and then, one may hear his name uttered respectfully, if somewhat *sotto voce*, in connection with his papers (the one we co-wrote was very well-received and continues to be taught in university classrooms around the world), the name, as you know, has only the most precarious relation to the thing, and this relation, like everything else that holds us together, only weakens with age. *Res et verba*—or is it *verbum*? No matter. As if in reaction to my present confinement, my imagination has expanded to such capacity that I can hold in my mind up to a dozen contradictory, half-baked, or simply wrong ideas at once, sometimes in several languages, with no internal discord or fatigue. At any rate, the spelunker's good, if undeserved, reputation persists, but this shouldn't surprise you, for you know all too well his ability to charm. Oh well, we all make mistakes, especially in our youth, and yours was glorious: your endless legs; the relentless way you drank with him at the graduate bar every night and then how the two of you would withdraw, hand in hand, making everyone else so melancholy; and not least, your flying hair! And how much of it you had! So thick, so curly—and me with my poor head in a scarf. Well, enough of that. Let me return to the point: My story which, in the right hands—and yours, need I even say so, are almost certainly the right ones, or will be, as soon as you deal with that little rash of yours—might even be parlayed into an award like the Nobel Prize. Or a Pushcart, at least. You see, despite being a dried-up geology professor, I do know about such things. So let me, at last, begin:

I bought a condominium here in Cambridge in, let me see, 1992, or thereabouts. It was one of those periods, not unknown on our campus, of technological lull, just after the massive investment in machine intelligence disappeared and just before all the previously empty office space began to fill, and then overfill, with men and women in neutral-colored polo shirts and credibly rumpled khaki pants yakking into their cell phones about positioning, experience economies, and the eternally *misterioso* thing known as *market cap*, which, despite appearances, is not something anyone could wear, although I am sure you will find a way to wrap this terrible pun around my head in your next publication. As I was saying, I had just bought my condo, and I was troubled to find, upon moving in, several things wrong with it. First, the plumbing. During my inaugural shower, I was interrupted by banging on my front door. Throwing my robe about me, I ran to answer the summons. My panic was only increased by the fact that I had not completed the paperwork on my fire insurance and, for that reason, I guiltily supposed the building was on fire. In this state of indignity, not to mention undress, I flung open my door to find, however, that the ruckus was due only to my female neighbor, who was hollering. TURN THE WATER OFF. TURN IT OFF. TURN THE GODDAMNED WATER OFF.

By taking a shower, I was flooding her apartment, three floors below!

I tightened my robe and returned to the bathroom. She followed close at my heels—to ensure my compliance, I suppose. I squelched the tap as she requested, but I could not resist wondering aloud: How was it that no one from the intervening apartments, on floors two and three, was up here complaining about the same problem? She explained that she'd always had trouble with leaks from my floor; the second and third floors, she said, worked like sponges, absorbing water for as long as they could until finally the sponges were overfull and the excess ran down her walls. Her firm grasp of the details of this extraordinary theory lent it a surprising credibility and I thought, either this woman is mad, or

I have made quite a poor real estate investment. I resolved then and there to re-grout the tub as soon as possible, as a stopgap, and to investigate the local physics later, when the bill from her painters arrived, just as she assured me, more than once, that it would.

Problem #2: the garden. Which was not a garden at all but a sort of catchment area into which the river would overflow after particularly heavy rain. I don't mind wetlands—after living in Key West for many years, dampness is hardly new to me—but the mosquitoes were intolerable. So, one afternoon during that golden semester, your first with us, I asked our spelunker, who as you may recall had a reputation for being handy, to build me a birdhouse that I could fill with fruit and install on the deck where I hoped it would attract members of a nearby colony of fruit bats. I had been told that the bats were useful for keeping the local mosquito population in check, as mosquitoes preferred the taste of fruit bats to that of people like you and me.

No doubt the bats are sweeter.

I'd seen the bats myself. One evening, I walked past a tree blanketed with quivering black leaves; as I drew near, their hundreds of lustrous wings rustled companionably and then, after I'd thrown a loose sidewalk brick in their direction, they beat the air into a black froth, overwhelming my exclamation, which escaped from my mouth just as the mass, as one, attained the air: *Die Fledermaus! Die Fledermaus!* An expression which seized me as so terrifically witty, I was compelled to bite my hand.

In due course, the spelunker arrived at my condominium, toolbox at the ready and, if I may say so, looking rather fetching in a pair of salmon-colored Bermuda shorts. Since I know you need certain details to make your story attractive to the prize committees, I will list them here and allow you to perform your artistry on them yourself (I can't do every-thing for you, after all): He had blue bug-eyes, a skin rash that looked a bit like your own, and, unusually for a man engaged in the so-called life of the mind, lovingly tended, if somewhat furry, quadriceps. Of course, even these details are not enough to make a character prize-worthy—for he still requires a name! For my own reasons, which I need not share with you, I shall avoid giving him a lyrical name and simply call him Eleven, to memorialize the fact that he was my eleventh (as *you* might say) a-man-u-en-sis—and here I confess that I ran, flushed with irritation, to the dictionary when you first used the word in your mid-term paper, for which, out of spite, I gave you a D, to remind you of the dictionary, and recommended that you seek the wisdom of George Orwell's fine essay on power trips and the English language.

For which bit of bitchiness I *do* apologize, as I told your mother yesterday. Perhaps by way of forgiveness-by-proxy, she bestowed upon me a thin-lipped smile and asked if I had any idea what was in the little white paper cups, and then she leaned upon her spade and grinned. (Your mother, I should tell you, has lately been seen digging on the near hillside at dawn, in defiance of the rule against roaming the grounds at odd hours). Speaking of homely implements like your mother's spade reminds me of something that I have long wanted to tell you: It was love at first whack for me and Eleven. No sooner had he begun construction on my bat house than he found, under a plank on the deck, a half-drowned river rat that he was obliged to kill with his drywall hammer, except that he missed and brought the instrument down on his thumb instead. I was obliged not only to kill the rat myself, which I did with the application of my heaviest Calphalon pan, but also to offer the spelunker ice, sympathy, and the aperitif he requested—a glass of sherry—even though it was not yet noon. Sitting on the couch, I boldly offered to kiss his boo-boo better. Yes, yes, "boo-boo" *was* exactly what I said, although I'm sure you'd do a better job with the dialogue, making my display of seductive motherliness seem at once gruesome and oddly sexy, as if I were playing Anne Bancroft to his Dustin Hoffman, except you'd give me away yet again by calling your result quote, The Graduate *Student*, unquote, cuckoo-ka-chew. Well, so what. Indulge me. For here I must follow my pleasure out to its natural, obvious, and, for all that, utterly delicious end: shortly I was kissing, passionately kissing, not just his boo-boo, but *him*.

You mean to say you didn't know? Well, it makes no difference after everything that has happened. Part of my problem in telling you this potentially very profitable story is that Eleven, the spelunker, is as misty to me now as the geological prehistory of, say, the Mediterranean basin, which was, not coincidentally, the subject of my first published paper, of which you made such fun of in your book. Which was all to the good, of course. All scientific research, even my own, early work, is worthless if it only sits on dusty library shelves. You, at least, have been kind enough to make use of it. Speaking of old books: When I try to imagine Eleven, what I remember most clearly has nothing to do with those few literary essentials I've already mentioned, but the simple odd fact that he had about him a peculiar smell, like that of a newspaper left out in the rain. If he'd been a different sort of person, more vain perhaps, I would have more to offer you here by way of memory: the precise texture of his awful skin, the position in which he preferred to sleep, how his fine hair felt when I pulled it out in clumps with my hands. Such were our ecstasies. As a literary person, I am sure you understand.

I'm also sure you know by now that, when Eleven and I started to see each other, I had already embarked on a project that I called geoliterature, a form of writing that would allow me to chart a course toward those happy shores of art where you have already anchored your stately boat, and enjoyed such good results (as your mud-streaked mother reminds me thrice daily, at least). Although I'd been working on my "geolit," as I like to call it, for some time before your arrival, it was only during your first semester in our program that I worked up the nerve to share some of my writing with Eleven. It was an operatic meditation on the geography of a coral reef in Key West as told by a woman singing a lament to its destruction by tourists. Eleven suggested he might help me by translating it into Russian, because he felt that the language and people who produced both Chernobyl and Nabokov might also be persuaded to accept, of all people, a literary geologist—that is to say, *me*. Naturally, I could not disagree. The day waned over his shoulder. Outside, as mosquitos buzzed near the lamp, which every now and then emitted a stinging *ZAP!* (the bat house was still, at this point, incomplete), Eleven continued to hold forth on my couch, adding that his sister-in-law, a literary agent in St. Petersburg, could probably help us get the translation published. *ZAP!* He wrote down her number on a scrap of paper. Thanking him, I imagined great things: The domes of Petersburg! Ziggurats! *ZAP! ZAP!* A Pushcart at last, and congrats, congrats! (Rats! Can they give me *nothing* for this infernal repetition?)

To make a long story short, or at least shorter, Eleven translated my Key West reverie, but with terrible results, as I learned when I gave the translation to a friend of mine, a native Russian speaker, who retranslated it back into English. Only then did I begin to understand the extent to which the spelunker had abominated my work. In the spelunker's hands—in his mouth—on his *tongue*—my tragic, elegiac vision had become—a farce! Not only was the story much shorter, but it contained whole new scenes of screeching women singing arias, slamming doors, and chasing men in loincloths, not to mention a fantastical tabby cat who took his day's entertainment biting the tails off Norwegian water rats which, being half-drowned by a recent flood, were at a pitiful disadvantage anyway. To top it off, the spelunker's translation included another new character who was—*quel surprise*—a Russian spelunker! This character got all the wittiest lines, many of which I'm sure you would recognize.

One night when Eleven said you were at the library, I broached the subject with him over more sherry. Our consumption was such that I was now obliged to buy it by the cask; his thumb had healed to the point that there was only a shadow of a bruise, and he only flinched slightly when I squeezed it. Although perhaps this is not what is meant by "healing," I felt sufficiently confident that I was not dealing with a delicate convalescent, and so I did not stint my criticism. To his credit, Eleven bore my remarks stoically and promised to revise. He drained his glass, placed it on the sideboard with a delicate movement of his hand, and left. (I kept the glass and did not wash it, for it still bore his prints and a faint powder along the rim, where his lips had touched it.)

I did not see him again for several weeks. He seemed to have forgotten his professional obligations: Students gathered for his classes only to disperse, confused and professorless; he failed to attend committee meetings where his presence was compulsory; his mail piled up in the mailroom; the department secretaries called his house and left numerous messages on his answering machine. On the phone, a West Coast professor mentioned to me in passing that he thought he'd seen the spelunker, but only hazily, from a distance, hanging grimly on a bungee cord on the mineral face of a ravine; a visiting poet said he'd spied Eleven shouting at a young woman who'd banged into his car after she barreled through a red light downtown at dusk; someone else, a woman, called me in the middle of the night to ask in a faint voice if he was there, to which I responded by gently resting the receiver in its cradle and extinguishing the light. In a final twist, I received in the mail a document purporting to be a copy of the revised translation, but the pile of paper emitted such noxious fumes that when I sat down to read, the letters drifted before my eyes in a dreadful-smelling chemical mist and then seemed to attain legs and intentions, whereupon they crept off the page as if embarrassed by their own stink. Before the pages dissolved in this way, however, I managed to read enough to understand that *this* translation was *also* terrible, but thanks to the chemicals, I was spared the details, and the only lasting effect was a migraine that took several hours to clear.

I had nearly given up on the spelunker when, one evening as I was backing my car out of my space in the faculty lot, I caught sight of him in my rear-view mirror. I cut the engine and jumped out. A crust of ice and salt crunched beneath my boots.

"Spelunker!" (Actually, I called him by his name.)

He raised his hand. The thumb still seemed slightly swollen. "Howdy!"

I ignored this childishness. "Where the hell have you been?"

The story that tumbled out of him was not interesting, so I shall not bore you by retelling it in detail. Suffice it to say, he'd left immediately for the library after departing from my apartment on that afternoon when I'd criticized his translation, but before he could install himself in his carrel, he was waylaid by a pack of students who by various stratagems convinced him to attend a party out of town. At one point, someone handed him a drink that caused him to feel sleepy, and he stretched out on a couch to rest. He woke, disoriented and ill, at a bus stop in Cincinnati, where by chance he had a friend who put him up for a few weeks while he recovered from this odd and, as he said, "defamiliarizing," experience.

I would have asked him why he didn't call, but I didn't want to seem like the incessant kind of woman who demands that sort of thing, and besides, by that time, we were leaned up together against a lamppost, his mouth was all over me, and I was hardly going to ruin the mood.

He stopped, and said softly: "I've hoked you up a bit of phony…"

"Telephony?" I was still hoping he would say why he didn't call.

"No!" He exhaled, gathered himself. "I've clapped a banger; talked a line; copped a whopper; fed you, you know, a slice of baloney," he said, examining my face with minute attention. "A thick one. But I must say, it seems not to have disagreed with you."

But he read me wrong—I was roiling, indignant. I pulled my lips over my cold teeth and suggested adjourning to my condo.

"Sure," he said.

Seated stiffly beside one another, our glasses of sherry balanced on the sofa's wide arms, we began again to talk. I had to know *everything*.

This was a mistake.

"I spent three weeks in Cincinnati with a woman I met on the bus. I don't know why I did it; she was a dead lay and a sloppy drunk. She worked in a record store—one of those retro-chic, all-vinyl joints—but the only thing I really liked about her was that she filched me a copy of Schubert's *Die Forelle*. The Deutsche Grammophon release."

As it turned out, I owned it. A copy, I mean. I teed it up on the turntable.

They say bad news can distort one's perception; perhaps that explains what happened next. In this composition, Schubert meant to approximate a burbling stream and the quiet fishy life within it. But that night, the sounds emanating from the record player seemed more like a reveille blown by a band of ravens, and it produced in me an overwhelming vertigo. I fell to the floor, writhing. My glass shattered on the parquet.

I spent the remainder of that night extracting the truth from him one dismaying pellet at a time. For I had conceived the idea that, if I could just understand what this other woman had that I lacked (hair, perhaps?), I could decide whether to adjust myself accordingly. After all, I only wanted to make Eleven happy, and anything she could give him, surely I could give double.

Well, he said, the first time he *did it*, he thought I wouldn't really mind, and he felt justified because he'd been so confused and hurt by my comments on his translation. The second time he felt like *doing it* was all right since he'd already *done it* once. After that, a curious economic sort of guilt overcame him and he became convinced that it would be best to *do it* as many times as he possibly could, figuring that the more he *did it*, the less valuable and significant each individual instance of *doing it* would become and, therefore, the less upset I would be.

After hearing this absurd provocation, I do not know why I persisted in my questioning, but I did, even going so far as to ask whether the woman wore glasses (yes), his impression of their heft (light, plastic), whether her hair was long or short (long), and whether he asked permission to unpin it (he did). I asked other questions, intimate ones that cannot be included in your volume if it is going to be printed at all, let alone considered for a National Book Award, and so I shall leave off here, excluding those details except for one: as I sat hunched at his feet, growing inwardly ever more detached, his speech merged with the rumor of bats tussling in my bat house (I had been obliged to finish it myself), the ominous squawks of the plumbing, and the susurrations of rodents settling to sleep behind the drywall. Perversely, the more he told me, the less I felt I *knew*—and yet, how much greater was my desire for knowledge! It was as if his confession had incapacitated my reason so badly that, like a severely burned person, I felt the most overwhelming thirst, one that was, however, only intensified by drinking. As he talked, I fingered the broken glass, pushing at the edges of the pooled sherry. He poured me a fresh drink that I consumed in tiny, angry sips.

Curiously, this intense question-and-answer session lent a kind of rejuvenating glue to our relationship, and we agreed, on the spur of the moment, to take a weekend trip to a beach town on the Cape where our mixed-up moods, alternating elation and melancholy, seemed mirrored in the behavior of the gulls, particularly in the way their enthusiastic banking and swooping contrasted bathetically with their sad cries.

The matter of the translation had not yet been laid to rest, however, and so, while we were unpacking in our hotel room, I ventured to inquire about it. After giving me a long look, to my surprise he produced the document from his bag and said he'd go for a walk on the beach while I read. If I needed him, he said, I should just "ping" his cell phone, and he would call me right back.

"Like bats," he smirked on his way out the door, just in case I didn't understand what he meant by this stupid locution, by his prissy little *ping, ping, ping.* "Like echolocation."

Outside, dusk descended, the seagulls swooped home to their nests, the lights went on in the cabins by the water, and several hours later, when I finally looked up from his manuscript, I realized that Eleven had not returned. I called the number he left but I kept getting disconnected. Panicked, I raced down to the waterfront and paced the water's edge, searching for his footprints. A hundred yards out, I discovered a worn brown glove, left-handed, that seemed familiar. I put it in my pocket. And that was the last I, or anyone else, saw of him.

It was too bad, not least because his translation was perfect. Too perfect—it was machinelike, demonic, mathematical in its precision, its rage for orderly clauses and *le mot juste.* Like a fire that has burned out the contents of a closed room, the translation was airless, and what I meant to tell him was that I wanted the old version back. The translation needed the oxygen of mistakes. Imperfection made it breathe.

When I returned to Boston, I was astonished to learn that the spelunker's house had been sold, and that he had lined up a replacement professor to cover his spring classes. It occurred to me then that he had intended all along to use our trip to make his escape. Chastened, I slunk around his neighborhood. On bad days when I could not restrain myself, I even checked to see if there was mail in his box after the postman had come and gone. No mail ever arrived for him, not even a grocery circular, although after a time letters began to arrive addressed to someone else entirely. I checked those too, just in case.

One day, in the course of this humiliating yet irresistible ritual, I found several intriguing items in the box, none of which was, strictly speaking, mail. There was a sentimental Polaroid of a woman holding a starfish as the sun set behind her on a beach, and another Polaroid of the same woman, this time in his apartment, eating a banana while half-undressed. I kept the photographs, but I hardly know if they belonged to the spelunker or the person who moved in after him. Perhaps they had been in the box, unnoticed, for years, and I had somehow missed them. No matter—I added them to the shoebox I keep full of such things, for no reason except to occasionally remind myself of the precise depth and breadth of the world's mystery.

Incidentally, I did telephone the St. Petersburg number to check on the literary agent. I got a machine; the mechanical voice advised me, in American English with a strong southern accent, to leave a number, and someone would ping me. *ZAP!* Rats.

One afternoon, I cornered the chairman of the department. It was mid-March. The last of the winter snow had melted, perfuming the air with the smell of mud, making my senses preternaturally acute. Indeed, for a moment I was sure I felt beneath the soles of my feet the movements of earthworms dredging the soil. The chair had lost weight, I noticed, in the course of the previous semester, and his eyes seemed oddly bright, feverish—which perhaps explains why, when I broached the subject of the spelunker, he insulted me by asking: "Did you really have to burn the place down?"

I protested my innocence. "You know how bad the housing is for non-tenured faculty," I said. "With all those books, his place was a firetrap anyway."

After that, the events leading to my confinement here followed in quick succession. The incident in the bath was the first. Of all the handy purposes to which the spelunker allowed me to put him, his assistance, so to speak, in re-grouting my bathtub was the most valuable. I was sitting in my bath admiring the grout when a scratching came from down below. The noise grew louder and more frenzied; the water rippled and sloshed over the sides, spattering the floor. As I leapt up, I caught my reflection in the mirror. My hair was dripping like a very Medusa. The drains in my apartment backed up, one after another. A wave of foul sludge washed into my toilet; I slammed the lid shut and sat down hard upon it, at which point the sink faucet sprang a massive leak. As I turned the valve to stop the flow, the handle fell off and water sprayed everywhere. Fearing a return of my crazed neighbor, I ran naked down four flights of stairs screaming for everyone in the building to turn off their water, for it had suddenly become clear to me that the suspension of the laws of physics enjoyed by the tenants on floors two and three had finally been extended to my apartment on the fourth floor, and now water was leaking upwards, and everyone in the building was now flooding *my* rooms.

Thus does myth erupt into history, which is not always up to the task of containment.

When I shared this story with your mother, she told me, between peals of laughter, something I did not know, namely that the inclusion of ash from human bones has long been the secret to making marvelous tiling cement.

And now I have a confession to make. About halfway through the semester, as I'm sure you recall, I had asked you to meet me in the glass observation booth above the seminar room in order to discuss your mid-term paper. You already knew the grade you'd received, and your wan, cowed face filled me with a wild pleasure that I tried hard to conceal as you noted our meeting in your calendar: "Obs Room, 4 pm. Topic: My Bad Grade." Of course, because I myself had failed to make note of the meeting, I forgot all about it. Sadly for you, late in the afternoon on the appointed day, I happened to see Eleven in the hallway outside the seminar room and, knowing the room was always empty at that hour, pulled him inside, where he proceeded to spelunk me right there on the table. I only remembered my meeting with you when, sitting up, I saw you through the window, sprinting down the embankment. Your mouth was hanging open for some reason, and as I recall you did not come again to class. Your final paper appeared in my mailbox at the end of the semester. I'm sure it was a masterpiece. Alas, you know how it is at the end of the semester. One never has enough time to read everything.

I wish to close by observing that, when I saw you last week walking on the lawn with your mother, you looked exactly as successful as your mother says you are. You've lost weight, and your new haircut suits you. Your mother seemed buoyed by your visit, so buoyed, in fact, that I believe she has finally made her escape, for the whole staff has been looking for her all morning, to no avail. Last night, it occurs to me now, she'd signaled her intent by making me a gift of her shovel, which I put to use immediately by beating out a fire that had started in a corner of a nearby hedge. People came running from all directions shouting what I believe were their congratulations, although I hardly knew what for. I ignored them and continued to strike the bushes, from which a great cloud of black birds rose to block the advance of my admirers. Something about the scene reminded me of Van Gogh's last melancholy landscape (do you know it?) in which three roads lead out from a yellow wheat field toward a horizon crowded by a murder—truly, there is no other word for it—of crows. Out, out, and out: there is something to be said for an imagination that admits of multiple exits. Finally, and on a more prosaic note, I should mention that during your last visit, you left a box of tiny sugar-pink rosebud candies at the front desk. Even though I couldn't make out what you'd scrawled on the label, I just knew they were meant for me. They were delicious. Thanks, and congrats.

I, Zinnia

Two summers ago, when my mother fell ill for the last time, I returned to Maple Bay to find the roses blown, the deadbolt broken, and a week's worth of newspapers piled against the door. A plate lay near the downspout beside a teacup containing a handful of rose petals and a stick. A dozen sterling spoons jutted from the lawn, which reflected greenly in their concavities. My father had called before he cleared out. My mother, he said, was in no shape to be alone. When I found a sticky highball glass on the mantelpiece, beside the dusty brandy decanter in which my father's handprint was just visible, I knew he was, at best, only half right. My mother was in no shape for *something*; perhaps he meant that I was her last chance to find the shape she'd had. Like mother, like daughter: my other, myself. As I was about to consign my father's dirty glass to the fireplace, I noticed an odd lump among the cinders which turned out to be a charred biography of Thor Heyerdahl, swollen by rain that had leaked in through the flue.

My mother was in the Florida room, rocking in her chair. She smelled like she was afraid of the bathtub again. I focused on my breathing.

"Zenobia?"

Though her voice was faint, and her tone credibly miserable, she still could piss me off with just a word.

"Your other daughter," I snapped, "will be here at the end of the week."

My mother closed her eyes, but I didn't disappear.

"That trick doesn't work anymore," I told her.

I ransacked the closet for a fresh robe. I found clean sheets and took those, too. No point in cleaning her up just to deposit her in a filthy bed. The bathtub tap opened with a squeal. Water pounded into the tub, first brown, then clear. I dumped in a container of anti-bacterial liquid soap that I'd discovered in the medicine cabinet. When I called my mother, she came right away and undressed without a word. This surprised me. I thought she'd at least try to call me Zenobia.

She lowered herself into the water where she flushed all the way to the old tattoo—a peace sign—on her arm.

"It's too hot."

"It's just the way you like it."

She opened the cold tap.

"You'll shock your system," I warned her. She muttered something I didn't catch, then snorted triumphantly when I stubbed my toe on my way out the door.

Later, after I'd combed her hair and wrapped it in a towel, I tried to settle her into bed. Every time I pushed her under the covers, she popped up again, straight as the fireplace poker, and fixed me with her schoolmarm's glare.

"Nighty-night, Mom," I said firmly.

She pushed back her sleeves. Her forearms were covered in angry scratches. That's when I remembered the soap in the bathwater. Anti-germ Dial is not exactly Oil of Olay.

I rifled through her nightstand and came up with a bottle of lotion. She rubbed it all over, wincing ostentatiously as she touched the irritated places.

"Grit," I informed her, "is the main part of integrity."

"Tell me something interesting," she said, leaning back. "You can do it if you try."

Her scratched forearms were slick with lotion.

"Why did you marry that man?"

"First you boil me like a lobster, then you ask me that?"

The inflammation on her arms had subsided slightly. Perhaps she'd not been boiled enough.

"The day before yesterday," I offered, "I quit work."

She rolled her eyes.

"Go to sleep," I told her, and turned out the light.

In fact, my mother's intuition had been correct. I did have news—two items, both more interesting than my job, which was just a dumb gig answering phones at a department store call center. First: I was fourteen weeks pregnant by a man who no longer returned my calls. Second: On my last day at work, I'd convinced a customer to give me her credit card and expiration over the phone.

"The system is down," I said. "Did you just try to buy a two-hundred-dollar pair of jeans at our online store?'

In the background, a baby squalled. "Are you going to tell my husband?"

"I'll put your order right through," I assured her, "if you'll just confirm the card number and the expiration."

A friend had pressed the card, and I was good to go.

MY MOTHER KNEW about crappy jobs. Years ago, she'd worked as a social studies teacher in the Mount Pleasant schools. In the Sixties, it was easy to get a job teaching in a rough district like Mount Pleasant. The only people who wanted to work there were the ones who didn't mind being told off by third-graders or having to bring their own chalk to class when the budget dried up. My mother hoped that if she stuck it out, she'd qualify to join the union. With union perks, she said, she would have been happy to keep her nose-pickers and their Crayolas until the day she cashed her first pension check. That's what she wanted: a union job with the summers off. It was the kind of life, my mother said, you could make a life out of.

About that time, she got her tattoo. As a child, when I'd catch a glimpse of it, the blood would zing in my ears. "Zinnia Zompa," she would say whenever she caught me looking, "don't you even dream of coming home with one of these." In photographs from this period, her butter-colored hair streams to her waist, and the blue circle of the tattoo is visible on her upper arm. In one of these photos, she holds me on one hip. I smile broadly, gripping a fistful of her hair. She looks like she has swallowed a watermelon. Zenobia's coming any minute, and I have no idea.

When I was small, my mother liked to tell stories about her life before I arrived. Back in those days, she said, a girl lived at home until her father marched her down the aisle. If a girl had a job, even a good one, it was assumed she'd give it up when the first baby came along. Someone had to take care of the house. If you absolutely couldn't stand living with your folks before you got married, you could try to find a landlord who'd rent you a place without your father's signature on the lease. In that case, you just needed to find roommates—all girls, of course.

This was exactly what my mother did. With a bundle of her teaching money for a deposit, along with her diploma and a letter from the school board attesting to her employability, she convinced Mrs. Recchia at the St. Dunstan Arms, an apartment building named after the patron saint of locksmiths, to rent her a three-bedroom on the first floor. She took one room, subletting the others to her two best friends, Marcy Brito and Della DeFelice.

The St. Dunstan Arms was nothing special—two stucco stories with fake half-timbering and a parking lot separated from the street by a chain that Mrs. Recchia locked at eleven o'clock sharp, seven nights a week. She didn't like "her girls," as she called unmarried women tenants, to stay out late, never mind taking a guest home. Mrs. Recchia was a real pill, my mother said. But if you bounced a check, she didn't evict you, and she didn't raise her rents.

Of the three roommates, Marcy had the grandest aspirations: She wanted to be a movie star. To pay for acting lessons, she waited tables at the Big Boy. She'd tell her customers, mostly traveling salesmen on their lunch breaks, about her Universal Studios ambitions: *A girl can dream, can't she?* The strategy paid, for they over-tipped every time—out of pity, my mother said, though it might have also been true belief, the recognition of a rare bargain, the chance to buy a portion of happiness with pocket change. Whatever the cause, her tips went way up. She eventually collected so much that she opened an account at the bank, where she'd charmed the manager into an extra half-point on her interest. That was Marcy.

Della was different. She worked as a stable girl at the park and gave riding lessons when the regular teacher was too busy. She didn't much like the job, but for a long time she never managed anything better. Although Della's aspirations were not as definite as Marcy's, Della did sometimes say that she wanted to see the world, and she kept a portrait of Alexandra David-Neel, the famous traveler, taped to her vanity. My mother once showed me a photograph of Della. She had a long face and a funny smile that showed a gap between her front teeth. She looked like she might whinny.

At the St. Dunstan, my mother and her friends sat around drinking tea, organizing Green Stamps, and dreaming up ways to twit Mrs. Recchia, like putting chewing gum in her clothesline crank or taking a crowbar to the driveway lock. Of course, there were love stories. Once, my mother told me, Marcy caught crabs from her steady, Mr. Sam, and happened to mention her misfortune on the party line. A second chain appeared in the parking lot, and Mrs. Recchia took to locking it even earlier. But Marcy, after all, *had* Mr. Sam, his crabs notwithstanding; he was handsome and, though a good fifteen years her senior, my mother said he looked just Marcy's age. Once the episode with the crabs was forgiven and forgotten—Mr. Sam claimed he caught them sleeping on a dirty mattress when he was in New Haven on business, and Marcy, astonishingly, believed him—Marcy spent her days sketching patterns for her wedding dress. It looked, in my mother's opinion, like it came right out of the wardrobe department of *where else but* Universal Studios.

As for horsey Della, my mother said she brought her man problems on herself. For one thing, she was picky: she turned down every suitor she couldn't imagine marrying, and she couldn't imagine marrying anyone shorter than she was, or less good-looking, or without his own car. At one point, of the exactly four guys in the neighborhood who met Della's standards, three were already married, and the fourth went right off the list as soon as he started squiring a leggy brunette around. "Nobody likes a girl who's so much piss and vinegar," my mother would say, years later, to me and Zenobia, adducing Della's misfortunes as evidence against our discovery, in middle school, of the aphrodisiac qualities of contempt. We flirted ruthlessly and competitively with the biology teacher, who obliged us by getting flustered, dropping his chalk at the bat of a few carefully mascara-ed eyelashes. But when he offered Zenobia a limp frog in formaldehyde, she fainted, whereas I lost myself in longing for a pickled frog of my own.

"You gotta kiss a lot of frogs," my mother said, in response to my confession of lovesickness over a cup of loose-leaf tea. She turned it over and read the dregs: a cat and an acorn. Good omens.

"I'm not kissing any frogs," I replied, unimpressed, and retreated to my room. It smelled of the formaldehyde that always stuck to my clothes on lab day.

Of course, aloofness had its consequences. Just as Zenobia received bad grades in biology and I received exactly zero frogs in formaldehyde, finicky Della spent her nights alone, reading travelogues by the light of the hallway lamp. Then Della met Brookes Ferry.

One afternoon, Della invoked the magic words: Brookes was *it*. He was *the one*. My mother glanced at Marcy, who wasn't quite buying *it* either. Della rushed on: She'd met this paragon of masculinity over the garbage pails, where he'd introduced himself. He was new around, trying to be neighborly, and asked if he might help her with the trash. Della agreed, and that's how it began, with a distasteful chore lightened by half. Marcy shrugged, unimpressed, but my mother opened the jug wine and they toasted their way to the bottom.

For a while it looked like Della had been right. Brookes called when he said he would and arrived for their dates, on time, with a carnation pinned to his lapel. Once, my mother recalled, he brought a half-dozen poems in a manila folder. Della swooned. When she recovered, she read the poems aloud to the other girls. My mother, who was fond of asking Della in the same breezy, disconcerting way that she would later ask me about my boyfriends, "Oh, he's obviously very nice, but is he really *the one*?"

Typically, when my mother asked this question, we'd be driving in her car. It would be late, and we'd have already exhausted our usual games, belting out the old-fashioned songs we knew by heart, roaring down the interstate with the windows open so the whole world could hear us shout: *Daisy, Daisy, give me your answer, do!* My mother would roll back the moon roof, and I'd fade out, waiting for the night to sing back. Zenobia meanwhile would be wiggling in the backseat, snickering behind her hand. My dreams, I suppose, were all over my face—dreams of the future, of jobs and boyfriends. I knew about Zenobia's dreams, too, but she'd sworn me to silence and, being earnest, I kept my promises, even to people like Zenobia who mostly broke theirs. When you're young it's easy to believe that virtue will be rewarded sooner or later. Then sooner becomes later, and you discover just how dumb you are. "But is he *the one*, Zinnia?" Zenobia would repeat, blowing my cover about some boy I was mooning over, as she poked her head into the front seat. I always clammed up while secretly hoping he *was* "the one," whatever that might be. I was never right.

Della had been a believer, too. I imagined her as some-one like me, prone to blushing in response to my mother's questions, inadvertently giving my mother the answer she'd been fishing for, and confirming her ever more securely in her belief that all the ambiguous signs the world sent her way (blushing, silence, clustered tea leaves) could be ren-dered comprehensible when filtered through her ideas about romance—which did not, I should add, extend to poems, given or received. My mother was hard like that. When I once asked her whether Brookes' poems were any good, she dismissed the question. "Who cares? They were good enough for Della."

So much for poetry.

Later that summer, about the time my mother met my father and started spending less time at the St. Dunstan, Mr. Sam moved to Connecticut without so much as a by-your-leave from Marcy, whose Pepsodent cheerfulness took a beating. She picked at her food, grouched if anyone wanted to play a record, and barely managed to drag herself to the Big Boy in time for her shifts. My mother taught summer school, trying to interest a roomful of sixth-graders in the history of exploration. Marcy, having nothing better to do, typed up my mother's ditto sheets about Magellan, Colum-bus, and her favorite, Thor Heyerdahl. Even though Marcy streaked the sheets with crying and had to do them over, my mother refused to stop her. Work, my mother said, was therapeutic. Then Marcy began to make up stories about Thor Heyerdahl, which she also included on the ditto sheets. My mother used to tell us these stories, reading off the old dittos at bedtime. Growing up, I believed that Heyerdahl was forced to darn his own socks while sailing alone on the open ocean and had to use a shower brush to get the suntan lotion to the place on his back that he couldn't reach, as Marcy typed blurrily, "all by his lonesome."

When Brookes stopped coming around, Della just took it as one more provocation. She spent her nights off on the stoop with Marcy, scheming to get Brookes back. With help from my father, who was handy, they amplified the ringer on the hallway telephone so if Brookes *happened* to call, Della could hear it from the steps, where she liked to sit just in case Brookes *happened* to walk by again on trash night. And wouldn't you know it, one night he did, holding hands with another girl. Della shut herself in the broom closet where she sobbed all night.

That might have been the end of it, except that by bringing the new girl around, he'd inadvertently given *both* Della and Marcy something new to chew on. Between Della and Marcy, the Question of Brookes became something of a game. They taped a map of the neighborhood to the wall and pushed tacks into it, tracking him like battlefield generals. Sometimes they pasted up snide notes: "Seemed fatter today." "Tried Burma-Shave." (How they figured this one, my mother had no idea.) One night, at the height of their investigation, the phone rang in the hallway. No one was on the line when my mother answered. Years later, she told me she was sure the caller had been Brookes. Of course, there was no way to know.

When Della finally started dating again, she had more success, or perhaps (as my mother thought) she'd just gotten wiser. The more a man fell in love with her, the harder she pushed him away. Perversely, most became even more smitten after she'd told them where to get off. If they persisted, she tried to fix them up with Marcy. Years later, whenever I came to my mother with a heartbreak of my own, she reminded me of Della. "They say you catch more flies with honey," my mother said, "but Della filled *her* dance card by dousing it with kerosene!"

"Ugh!" I was in the car with Zenobia and my mother was giving us another lecture. I lit a cigarette, a habit I'd recently acquired. My mother frowned at me sideways, without looking away from the road, and rolled down her window.

From the backseat Zenobia said, "That's my Zippo."

"No, it's not!" I lied.

With her arm, Zenobia trapped my neck against the headrest. I felt my eyes bulge.

"Give it back!"

The cigarette hit the floor mat.

"Girls!" shouted my mother as she spun into the Big Boy's parking lot. Zenobia slammed against the back seat. In the side-view mirror, she was pinch-faced with rage. I retrieved my cigarette, re-lit it, and exhaled slowly, grinning.

"What I am trying to tell you," my mother said, her fingernails biting into the steering wheel, "is that it is better to be loved than to love."

I said, "That's just how the Venus flytrap works."

"You'll never go wrong," my mother replied, "taking your inspiration from nature."

Throughout the St. Dunstan melodrama, my mother taught her classes. Her unit on Thor Heyerdahl became an obsession. She dreamed up projects like making hand-stitched captains' logs and homemade hardtack, lessons she repeated with Zenobia and me. We built miniature replicas of Heyerdahl's balsa wood boats and listened to tape-recorded stories of his trips to the Maldives and the Sea of Azov. We even watched the documentary he'd made while sailing across the Pacific in the Kon-Tiki. When Thor reached to grab a wayward rope, something flashed in the gap of his short-shorts.

"They're not wearing very much, are they?" my mother remarked from deep within my father's easy chair. Zenobia bit her knuckle, stifling a laugh. I sat blushing until Heyerdahl changed the subject. There was a good possibility, he reported in voice-over while the camera closed on a dark fin sticking out of the water, that their ship would be capsized by a whale.

My mother always said Della had it coming. She should never have focused Marcy's attention on Brookes without considering the consequences. Naturally, Della cut Marcy off. She destroyed their map and hammered the tacks into Marcy's heirloom four-poster. To keep the peace, my mother made herself the go-between. Marcy told her to tell Della how much she owed for utilities; Della told my mother to tell Marcy she'd write a check. In the spring, Marcy announced that she was pregnant with Brookes's baby. Della cried through Easter week. My mother concluded another unit on Thor Heyerdahl by taking her class to the beach where they released popsicle-stick Kon-Tikis into the ocean. Della put a message to Brookes in one of the rafts, as if the gesture might make a difference. In an unexpected way, it did. After relinquishing her wish about Brookes to the sea, Della returned to the St. Dunstan with an offer to help Marcy alter her wedding gown. Nothing in the shops could accommodate her belly. Della said she was handy with a needle, though no one had ever seen her do more than darn a sock.

The peace, such as it was, did not last. The shrieks and slamming doors so vexed my mother, who'd gotten engaged over the course of that difficult winter, that she fled back to her parents' house where she became so busy with preparations for her own wedding that she stopped taking calls from the Mount Pleasant school system and forgot all about her union job and her curriculum on Thor Heyerdahl. She moved to the suburb of Maple Bay with my father, where she kept the house in which she mislaid her ambitions. Perhaps "mislaid" is not the right word for what my mother did with the lesson plan of her life. She *might* have mislaid it, or she might have done something more knowingly self-destructive, like locking it in the cupboard, or setting it adrift on a balsa wood raft bound for the Mariana Trench. Trying to find the right word is like looking into the sun. I have to close my eyes, and when I do, my vision is littered with bright afterimages of popsicle-stick Kon-Tikis.

YEARS AFTER MOVING to Maple Bay, on a summer morning when Zenobia and I were eating breakfast, my mother got a letter from Marcy, postmarked Miami. Brookes was long gone, Marcy reported, and not only had she lost the baby, but the miscarriage had been Della's fault because Della had stabbed her with a pin while putting up the hem of her wedding dress. My mother almost couldn't read for laughing. When she reached the end of the letter, she thumped the table, upending her fruit cup. The syrup ran down Zenobia's bare leg.

"Jesus, Mom."

"Sorry," my mother said, wiping her eyes.

"I don't understand what's so funny," I said.

"Of course you don't. Zenobia is the one with the sense of humor."

"Seafood!" Zenobia shouted as she punched my arm. On her tongue were bits of canned fruit.

"Shut your mother," I told her, meaning her mouth.

My mother replied to Marcy in a letter I read later when no one was looking. She told Marcy she was sorry about her sad news. The pinprick business, she wrote, sounded like sharp practice indeed.

Della's life went on, as lives do. She made a point of cultivating my mother, inviting her and my father along on her dates. They usually headed for the drive-in, all four of them bouncing around in her Chevelle. Back in Maple Bay, someone else put Zenobia and me to bed. My mother has told me that when she and my father went on these double-dates, they never talked about Marcy, although Brookes came up once or twice in conversation. He still lived nearby and, Della said, took his neighborly walks in the evening. I have one memory from this time: Zenobia is wailing in her crib, and I am saying, "Shut up, shut up, shut up," which may have been the only words I knew. It seems to me now that they might have been the only words I ever needed.

For his part, my father maintained that things between Della and Brookes had never been as cool as they seemed. Della was still following Brookes around, and he still took Della out now and then. I suppose my father heard stories at the garage where he worked with a group of guys from the neighborhood, alert, watchful types who liked to know the score. My mother disagreed. It was all rumors, she said. My mother told me that this argument continued through her pregnancy with me, right down to the isolated final weeks when Della came over to help let out my mother's maternity things. If, during these visits, she poked my mother with a pin, it did no harm, for I arrived in due time, a good-sized, healthy baby. My mother was disappointed when Della failed to visit after my birth. She'd almost given up on the friendship when the news came that, on the day I was born, someone had pushed Della into the path of the Dyer Avenue trolley, which ran right over her, breaking both her legs.

"That's what happens," my mother always said when she got to this part of the story, "when you try to have your cake and eat it, too."

In my christening photos, Della leans on her crutches and strains to smile. She looks as if she'd give anything to be somewhere else. After she recovered, she landed a job that required her to travel. She sent us postcards from the road, keeping my mother perpetually wondering what she'd missed by getting married and settling down. Eventually Della went as far as Nepal, where she set up schools for children who wore pieces of old tires on their feet instead of shoes, or so I gathered, at least, from the blurry photos she sent to my mother. My mother grimly reminded us of these children whenever we kicked our expensive sneakers against the front seat of the car while she was driving.

One of Della's dispatches arrived on the day every television station carried the news that Thor Heyerdahl had burned one of his boats, the *Tigris*, near Djibouti.

"Djibouti," my mother murmured, fanning the postcard over her chest as if she, too, might combust.

It was dinner time. We were seated around the table. The television was on; there was Thor Heyerdahl in his short-shorts, reclining on the deck of the Tigris. My father sliced his pork chop into strips, asking, "Where the hell is Djibouti?"

"Maybe that's where Della will wind up next," Zenobia said around a mouthful of pork chop.

"Oh, please," my father said.

"Oh, please," I sang, "please, oh please, pass the salad."

My mother glared.

I began to name all the other places whose names I knew in Africa: Cape Town, Pretoria, Addis Ababa.

"And the forty thieves!" Zenobia shouted, spitting pork chop everywhere.

There was pork chop on my face. "That's not what I said!"

Zenobia waved her knife at me while my mother asked my father why he always had to be such a moron.

"That's right," I said. "And I don't see what's so funny about Zenobia's remark, either."

"You," my mother said to me, "shut up."

We finished our dinner in silence broken only by the noise of the televised wind in the flaming sails of the *Tigris*.

I thought that postcard was the last we would hear of Della. It wasn't, not quite. When her father died, she inherited enough to buy a brownstone in Boston, where we visited her several times. Not only was she solicitous of me and Zenobia, but she always kept treats around for my mother, things that were not available in the grocery store in Maple Bay, like high-end coffee or gourmet caramel corn, the kind called "poppycock," which came in a can. We also continued to receive postcards from Della, and every year she sent me and Zenobia expensive gifts, fancy pop-up books or toys made of real wood, not plastic, on our birthdays.

Della got married the year I turned eleven. She looked elegant in a sheath of white silk, and the groom smoked a cheroot, which I found mysterious and even dashing. At the reception, the caterer served platters of deviled eggs; Zenobia ate too many and threw up in the car on the way home. Later, Della came to stay with us because the man upon whom she'd staked so much had, in the end, cleaned out her bank account before pulling a Houdini. During that visit, Della told my mother she wished she'd married a good man like my father. At first, I think my mother was flattered. She didn't have Della's fancy career or her passport covered with stamps. But Della's flattery soured, and my mother accused Della of wanting to steal my father, a paranoid fantasy I later recognized as the first sign of her present illness. After that, Della's letters arrived less frequently, and no more presents came in the mail.

Eventually, Brookes went to jail for what Della said he did, and my mother did not hear from Marcy or Della again, except for one letter she received while I was in college. I discovered the letter much later as I was packing up her things for Goodwill and my father was ringing lawyers all over town, preparing to sell the house in Maple Bay. In this letter, Marcy said nothing of Brookes, or the pinprick that caused her miscarriage. If she'd heard of Della's "accident," or of Brookes getting sent up the river, she didn't let on—a nuance I appreciated. I had just avoided a jail term myself, in much the same way, having finally learned to keep my trap shut. "I am happy to report," Marcy wrote, "that I am enjoying myself here in Miami. But I do miss our evenings at the St. Dunstan."

I later showed the letter to Zenobia, who had been rocking the baby. I smoothed the hair on her forehead; she cooed. Tonya was precious, not least because she was all mine.

"Baloney," Zenobia sniffed when she was done reading.

I don't believe my mother ever replied to Marcy's letter. I kept it, though, just in case. Someday I might understand things differently, and the letter might be a clue. Probably not, but you never know.

THE WEEK WITH MY MOTHER passed slowly. While my mother slept, or rocked in the Florida room, I baited mouse-traps and opened roach motels under the sink. Nights I searched the house for things worth saving. I didn't find much. In the back of the pantry closet, there was a pepper mill shaped like an apple. I remembered my mother telling Zenobia to twist the stem, so that pepper flakes fell into the palm of her hand. Zenobia cried when one of them got in her eye. In the cupboard, I found the broken toaster that my father refused to replace. "You'll electrocute yourself," my mother would tell me whenever I went fishing for my English muffin with a fork. She would take the fork away, but Zenobia was always ready with another one, egging me on. On the cupboard's high shelf, which I could only reach with a stepstool, I found a jar of milk teeth, presumably mine and Zenobia's.

"Plant them in the garden," my mother said from some-where over my shoulder. "You never know what might pop up."

"Jesus!" The stepstool creaked as I toed my way down. "I should put a bell on you."

"You want to wring my neck?"

Those spoons in the yard. What had she buried beneath them?

On our last day together, I took my mother to lunch at the Big Boy. She had been on a tiresome edge all morning, going on about the treacheries of Marcy and Della as if the contretemps with Brookes had happened yesterday. I tried to remember that her short-term memory was failing, her sense of time all but collapsed. This compassionate view didn't get me very far, and by the time we got to lunch, the only thing that kept me from strangling her was the prospect of having some fun with the ersatz credit card in my wallet. I was ready to make a mess.

"That Marcy Brito," my mother declared as the waitress distributed menus, "was a poor thing. She got herself knocked up, and she couldn't hang onto the father, either."

Her tone was bitterly delighted; she had Marcy all figured out. I adjusted my napkin in my lap. "Maybe it's not for us to judge, Mom."

"It's not for us to judge," she mimicked me, glancing sharply at my stomach. "Oh, Zinnia," she sighed. "How the mighty have fallen."

My mother ordered a salad and a Diet Coke. I asked for the same, to keep things simple. Our meals came right away. The cold soda hurt my teeth, so I asked for coffee to go and the check. The waitress took the card and disappeared.

My mother and I ate our salads in silence. I took my time, trying to make sense of my mother's "poor thing" remark, which I didn't agree with at all. Marcy's story didn't have to end badly. I pictured Marcy working a diner counter, chatting up businessmen during her break. Or she might be at this very moment at the helm of an airboat in the Everglades, bossing around her traveling companions just like Alexandra David-Neel. Or Thor Heyerdahl. Or Della herself, for that matter.

Or maybe that was just me, wanting to do that.

"Did Brookes really do it, Mom?" I tried not to sound as childish as I felt.

Wearing an expression that suggested that I just might be the most boring person on Earth, my mother speared a tomato with her fork. "You're just like your father. So invested in what's real."

"Unlike him," I reminded her, "I'm still here."

The waitress returned. The card had gone through. I signed Zenobia's name on the slip, just for fun.

I put my mother in the bath again later, using the terrible soap. She raised an eyebrow when she saw the bottle, but I was adamant: "Get in." As she sank, I felt a tiny triumph, but it was undercut by the sigh she emitted as she slid beneath the bubbles. She knew exactly what I was doing and why. She'd been just the same at my age, except that at my age, she was doing it better. I left her in the tub. I thought, *Drown, if you want to.* Afterwards, my mother fell asleep in bed. I stood at her door and watched her, aware that I was still not seeing her exactly but only the shadows she left around to frustrate me, like the spoons in the yard, which were too valuable to leave outside, but I couldn't collect them because then we'd lose the map to whatever she'd buried underneath. Now and then, she scratched herself. I tiptoed to the living room where I extracted the Heyerdahl biography from the fireplace. I pressed my palm against the damp cover, and I thought of Della typing up her homespun fantasies on my mother's ditto sheets. Had she tried to burn those, too? All I found in the fireplace were ashes. I put the book back and wandered to the kitchen. My mother's memories of nights at the St. Dunstan breezed the sails of my ears. An engine thrummed in the driveway. Through the window I saw Zenobia emerge from a taxi. She was lighting a cigarette and talking on her cell phone in her professional voice: "Whatever floats your boat." Her assistant followed, clipboard in hand. The taxi driver was shouting. No one had paid him. I ran out of the house, pushing past my mother, who was standing at the door, dressed, alert and, unbelievably, made-up.

"Zenobia!" she called.

My sister frowned and pointed to her ear, as if to say, *Can't you see I'm on the phone?* No doubt the roaming charges, like everything else about Zenobia, beggared imagination. The driver insisted on a double fare for going out to Maple Bay and back. I pulled my wallet from my pocket. I was pretty sure I had enough cash. In the distance, a siren wailed. I shivered, then got in. As the cab pulled away, I turned around. The sun was setting. My mother's spoons glinted on the lawn. *At least*, I thought, *I am getting somewhere.*

The Last of the Nuba

I MET HOLLY IN DECEMBER, after she'd exhausted the regular staff on the burn ward. She wasn't burned, but she
suffered from a wasting disease that had attacked the blood
vessels in her leg, requiring its amputation below the knee.
The amputation was a rear-guard action against an illness
that would never be definitively diagnosed, but had already
destroyed the cartilage in her nose, whose collapse lent her
face an infantile aspect, and her outer ears, which flopped at
the tips, pushing through her thin, pale hair. The amputation
scar was coming in reluctantly; to speed things along, her
doctor ordered regular debridement, a procedure that landed
Holly in the burn unit where persuading scars to form was
something of a specialty.

I was the ward's psychiatric liaison, for the scars that were
inside.

In the late 1970s, I was a young doctor dealing somewhat
arrogantly with my first patients—fallible bodies plainly
ensouled, whose enthusiasms enlivened my existence and
whose excesses were easy enough to manage when I bran-
dished my prescription pad and shot my cuffs in my white
coat. I could order electroshock, wet packs, straitjackets,
haloperidol. I could order nurses around, even late at night.
Perhaps especially, late at night. I was twenty-nine and cocky,
for all the usual disappointing reasons. My supervisor, an

insectiform tissue-graft specialist innocent of even the most basic ideas about psychology, chirped that I reminded him of a captain he once knew in the merchant marine, on the verge of botching his first command. Had I forgotten, he asked, as I struggled not to squirm under his twitchy gaze, that I had yet to lose a patient? *But,* I replied—as he raised a skeptical eyebrow whose longer hairs resembled nothing so much as antennae—*dying is just one of those things patients do.* To my newbie clinician's mind, it was like the first time you have sex: the question is not who, or even whether, but when. Of course I had no idea what I was talking about. The first patient who dies on your watch lives forever in your mind, a scorching reminder of everything you have failed to be. And in psychiatry, where our tools at this time were so few, dead patients often seemed to be entirely one's own crass fault—the suicides, particularly. Holly was my first immortal. She didn't commit suicide. I didn't kill her. But like anyone else in this business, I have my share of blood on my hands.

DURING HER DEBRIDEMENTS, Holly had a lot of pain but no one could get her on even the simplest of med regimens and so it went: her pain was allowed to reach a pitch, after which she received emergency doses of morphine, so that she was either screamingly under-medicated or nearly comatose. In brief lucid moments between these extremes, Holly worked at macramé and paged through the old magazines—*National Geographic* was a favorite—that tended to collect in the common areas. Half the nursing staff thought Holly had no right to howl over her limited wound when so many others on the unit were so much more extensively damaged. The rest blamed Holly's mother, Juliet, who did tend to haunt the nurses' station when Holly was enduring the worst of it, though I never noticed any unpleasantness in Juliet's behavior. The split on the ward did not quite conceal the fact that Holly was in danger from both sides. Half the staff wanted to kill her, and expressed their sadism by limiting her meds. The other half, who also wanted to kill her, expressed their murderous impulses by subtly pressuring her primary doctor to increase the morphine to quite unorthodox doses. The quisling did whatever he could to keep the loudest voices quiet—and I don't discount the ones in his head—on that particular day. But, as I told my supervisor, anyone could tell that the girl's psychology was not the problem. What she needed was an *advocate*—I admit my voice rose here, I was more easily moved to self-righteousness in those days—whose position vis-à-vis the staff would eliminate any question of entitlement, claims of specialness, or demands to jump the queue. With my help, which I planned to offer in the form of thrice-weekly hypnosis sessions— during which I imagined Holly, supine on my sofa, gazing alternately at the ceiling, at the spot where her foot used to be, and increasingly beseechingly at me—she could learn to endure her pain, earning the respect of the ward nurses, who would in turn feel free, if "free" is the right word for it, to medicate her sensibly.

"A little pain now for less later," I told my supervisor, who had grown very still. "That's the lesson I'll impart."

"Give it a try," he said finally. "*We* can't seem to do anything for her. Maybe your approach will shake something loose. God knows, we've tried everything else."

The ease with which we reached this agreement should have been the first clue that I was not fully in control of this case—which is to say, of my own contribution to it. Holly came for six sessions, during which I encouraged her to elaborate on a fantasy in which she lounged on a warm beach, and taught her to call this fantasy to mind whenever the nurses were too rough with her stump. She did this, which had the effect of keeping her quieter during debridements, and the nurses, admiring her new fortitude, did a better job with her meds. In other words, we'd achieved a triumph of publicity. As for what else we accomplished—well, I can see the truth more clearly now that so much time has passed. As is usual in cases of physician over-involvement, when I was depriving my patient of pain medication, I was avoiding a deprivation of my own.

When I met Holly, I was dating a policy analyst whom I wanted very much to marry. Annie and I were only three months into our courtship when I proposed. This antsy neuroticism was just the leading edge of my failings, which included a persistent slight aversion to sex, a prissiness about sounds and smells that I still had not completely overcome, despite two years' worth of sessions with a tight-lipped analyst whose withering interpretations had gradually rendered me less prone to withering in more fraught contexts. I should add that Annie was pretty—far more attractive a woman than I had any right to hope for. Perhaps not surprisingly, she did not feel quite the same urgent desire to marry me. But she was not a generally urgent person. That was one of the things I liked about her. She specialized in analyses of high-tech medical interventions whose cost was difficult to justify to the bean-counters in government and insurance—serious, deliberate work. Nights after my shifts, usually thirty-six straight hours on the burn unit, I was as vulnerable to Annie's calm numeracy as a lamb to the knife. Peeking at her through the curtains as I slipped my key in the lock, I found her singularly winsome: a petite brunette applying herself to her paperwork as she sat in the pooled light of my old gooseneck lamp, her glasses setting like dual suns as they slid down her nose. She would push her glasses up, re-knot her hair with whatever was handy—a pencil, a chopstick from her take-out dinner—and smile: *Hello, darling.* She was a goddess of the ordinary, of things that happened every other minute and could therefore be counted on to exhibit certain regularities. Whereas my days were full of unrepeatables like Holly, who were going through things, like their own dying, that would not re-occur in the history of the universe. For them, at least. Though it is surprising how many people die alone, or would, were it not for their doctors sitting at the bedside, listening in. That is a data set no one has counted up, to my knowledge.

"You're overreacting," Annie complained when I told her this. She was speaking into my armpit, half-asleep after we'd made the sort of tender, exhausted love that I was capable of after my shift and at no other time. We'd failed to draw the shades, and Annie was burnished head to toe in the weak light that reflected off the snow accumulating outside. "People die by themselves all the time. Think of marriage. By definition, half of every couple dies alone."

She leaned over and drew the shade, thrusting both of us into the room's shadows, choosing the darkness instead of allowing it to swallow us up. As if we might have a choice. As if anyone did.

"To hear you talk, you'd think dying was just some ordinary thing people do."

Annie pressed her lips together, making of her mouth a thin, refusing line. I murmured an apology; I hadn't meant to sound dismissive. My analyst had warned me about my tendency to let my speech outrun my intentions.

"If you are indeed my destiny," she continued, reminding me that my ring was still not quite around her finger, "then God has a wicked sense of humor."

"We make our own fates, Annie," I said, aiming for kindness because I didn't need to top a long day with a fight. I was surprised, as well, to hear Annie talk about destiny. I thought only primitive people still believed in things like that. "Besides, the law of large numbers would suggest that you're likely to marry *someone* sooner or later anyway. Why shouldn't it be me?"

"You're arrogant," she informed me, pulling the duvet up. Of course, she meant *supercilious*. But rather than correcting her, which would only have confirmed her impression, I reached instead for her feet and began to knead them, rolling my knuckles against the soles. At her office, fancy high-heeled shoes were sartorially de rigeur, which meant her days often ended with foot cramps. Unkinking these knots was an easy way to help her unwind. Mercifully, it didn't require me to say much. "But don't worry," she sighed, and I felt a knotted muscle release. "The law of large numbers only restates, in formal mathematical terms, what we already know from ordinary, non-mathematical experience."

"What's that?" I switched to the other foot.

"What goes around comes around. Karma's a bitch."

A policy analyst. A night nurse.

She pointed and flexed, leaning back so I could get a better grip. I chafed her pinky toes, which were colder than the rest of her. A blister had burst on one of them, leaving little shreds of flesh that I rolled gently back and forth.

"Is marriage always a tragedy?" I asked, to distract her from whatever discomfort I might have been causing her, or not. The skin was dead, after all.

"What do you think? Husbands usually die first. That's demography for you. Ouch. Facts."

"Facts," I echoed. She had shut her eyes. Her death's head look was not unappealing. I struggled against an urge to pinch off an especially resistant bit of old blister. The idea that I might have been repeating my workday experiences with Holly shimmered at some distant outpost of my consciousness. This was not tenderness. This was me, stupidly allowing work to bleed into my private life. I took my hands off her. "Say," I ventured, as it was time to change the subject, "did you read that book I gave you?"

It was a new novel by an author we both admired. I hadn't read it, which was a mistake. As it turned out, the book described the unraveling of a marriage.

"You want to let me know what I'm in for." She scooted to the nightstand and rummaged until she came up with the volume, which she handed to me as if it had never been my gift to her but something disappointing that she'd only borrowed. "Maybe you should read it."

Naturally I was crushed, though not so much that I could not appreciate the social adroitness of this move, which kept me uneasy as I juggled my doubts and hopes. At least she'd read it—cover to cover, it seemed, as there was a lot of underlining in a blue pencil she usually reserved for editing quarterly reports. Pictured on the back was the author, a pasty man leaning against New England-style clapboards that announced his respectability. Possibly I'd wanted to suggest something similar about myself. I slipped the book between the mattress and the box spring, resolving to look at it later, when I would seek and likely find some small hope for our relationship in her scrawled marks, despite her overt rejection. That's my job, as a psychiatrist: doubting that any story is the whole story. Of course, the book didn't make her uneasy; *I* did. But wasn't that marriage's whole point, to find someone with whom to sound the limits of one's uneasiness, in order to outgrow them?

A FEW DAYS LATER, Holly's mother called with news: Holly was off the burn unit. The wound had finally granulated in. But she was having nightmares. All night, every night, dream-Holly lay immobilized on a marble bier, while a nurse pulled her toenails out with a pair of pliers. Sometimes Holly was made of butter, and the nurse had a pastry torch.

"She's bedridden," Juliet continued. "Her aorta could go any time. Can you come out?"

"Of course," I told her. My rotation on the burn unit was ending soon. I had no other commitments. I was glad to be of use.

I arrived to find Juliet was in the midst of an argument with a neighbor, a young woman whose face might have been striking, had it not been thoroughly smudged with soot from the leaves she'd been burning in the yard. The problem, Holly's mother informed me, was that the bonfire made Holly cough, putting pressure on her fragile aorta.

Juliet said to the neighbor, "This man is a doctor, Lola. He'll tell you."

The woman named Lola wore yellow Wellington boots and a barn jacket that closed with toggle buttons. She brushed a flyaway hair from her face and thrust out a hand for me to shake. No ring on her finger. She met my eyes and I drew back, as if I'd received a mild electrical jolt.

"It's that time of year," Lola pleaded, though it hadn't been "that time of year" for weeks. "The leaves dropped late. Everyone's doing it."

Holly's mother had stepped away. Out of the corner of my eye, I could have sworn I saw her smiling. How intrusive, to engage me in matchmaking while I was trying to offer psychiatric treatment to her daughter. Perhaps the nurses had been right about her after all.

"Put it out," I snapped. "Doctor's orders."

Lola flashed a look that told me she would do as I said, but that I would be wrong to infer much beyond politeness from her acquiescence. Of course, her silence left me free to infer a great deal, and I can see now that here was the key to Lola's influence, the ease with which she could unmoor me from my familiar perspective, lift the ropes and give me a push that set me to dreaming like a toy boat loosed into the sea. Against my own wishes, to remain coolly unflappable, professional, sturdy and dependable, as would befit a *practically* practically-married man, I smiled, pleased as—

"A late lunch?" she offered. "I have enough for two. Tomato soup, with cheese toasts."

"Raincheck." Inclining my head toward Holly's mother who was still loitering by the front door, I pulled out a business card and handed it to Lola. "Duty calls."

She slid the card into a pocket. "Do you ever call back?"

I smiled again, to mark the end of the interview, and headed inside to do my damned job.

Holly's cluttered house unsettled me. Plants of all sorts, in bright ceramic pots or else hanging from the ceiling in macramé hammocks, filled the interior to the glassed-in solarium at the back. In the dining room, the table was set for seven—the whole family, including Holly, who could not possibly rise for the meal—with sturdy blue plates on Bonnard yellow placemats. Because Holly was too ill to be moved, I was to see her in the living room where a bed had been made up. Distressingly, the room had no door. Our sessions were to occur in the midst of family life, with her four younger siblings running in and out while Juliet puttered among the plants. Try as I might, I could not tell the children apart. They were all variations on the same tow-headed, jam-smeared theme, preoccupied with mislaid shoes and lost homework. It was a home in which it was easy to disappear. I folded myself into an armchair, pulled out my notebook, and readied my pen. Across from me, calmly recumbent in the eye of all this activity, Holly looked up from her macramé. *Hey, Dr. Teller.*

She told me about her nightmares, which were like the children in their infernal similarity: she fell to pieces like a fillo sweet, she disarticulated like a chicken that her mother might ask the butcher to cut up. As was appropriate for a young woman of limited experience, her associations suggested the safe suburban universe of the meat counter and the bakery aisle. She relayed her dreams lightly, all the while making loops with her macramé. Perhaps she was too immature to fully apprehend her own circumstances—she was simply too young to die, to grasp the concept. At once I understood my new task: to reconcile her, not to her ordinariness, as on the burn unit, but to her death. I told her as much, but she only shrugged, a move that dislodged the loose shoulder of her nightgown. With her long fingers she worked the cream-colored string. That day, instead of analyzing her nightmares, I told her that they were a common side effect of the drug she'd been given at the hospital. With disgust I heard myself speak—I was not exactly lying, but I was avoiding the more difficult subject of her vastly foreshortened life, which now included the awareness that certain things, such as drooping peignoirs and their ordinary sequelae, would never be hers.

She said, too brightly: "So that's that, then." Another little shrug, another inch of fabric slipping away.

"I suppose," I replied, struggling not to reach across the space between us and quell my anxiety by covering the shoulder that was now fully exposed. But when Holly left off her macramé in order to pull up the fabric by herself, my guilt was enormous. She was letting me know that she wouldn't ask me to do deep work if I was not up for it. Wouldn't ask me to get too close if the prospect repelled me. She was only a girl doing macramé, after all. "We can certainly talk about the meanings of these things," I told her, contritely.

She nodded, absorbed in her macramé.

ANNIE WENT AWAY for a month, traveling around the country on a project for a national children's health organization. In her absence I had nothing to do but check in on the regular outpatient ward and consult on cases as the need arose, which it did not often. I even had time to wonder about the wisdom of my proposal to Annie, who had come, suddenly, to bore me. She called every few days in order to squawk reports from her latest research into my ear. I permitted her to ramble, even encouraged it. I didn't want to cut her loose without knowing more about how and why she had suddenly turned out to be inadequate. All my training suggested that the fault was likely to be my own; there was nothing particularly wrong with Annie. So I squelched my annoyance, and tried to treat her with the consideration that I imagined would befit a future wife. Mine, I mean. Perhaps I found Annie boring because although I continued to see Holly on our usual twice-a-week schedule, certain developments on that front had shifted the distribution of my interests. Still, the precise point of transition remained obscure. All I know is that one day, as I was arriving for my session with Holly, the neighbor Lola came running down the walk. Thick black smoke billowed from her doorway. She was slightly knock-kneed in her rubber boots, and wearing a pair of elbow-length oven mitts. She handed me a fire extinguisher and ran away, into the burning house. *Ladybug, ladybug*, I thought, mindlessly, as I ran after her, not wanting to feel whatever I was feeling, on seeing her again.

Inside the house, the oven door lay open to reveal a fire-licked interior and, at the center, a beautiful pound cake that looked just about done. I pulled the safety on the extinguisher and motioned for Lola to step back. But she came toward me instead, an awkward woman with her arms encased in oven mitts.

"My cake!"

"Is on fire." I cocked the extinguisher's trigger.

"Not the cake! Just the oven." She reached into the flames.

"Lola!" I saw the burn unit, heard Holly's screams. "Stand back!"

I shut my eyes and shot for what seemed like an hour. The fire fizzled. The wind blew through the house, clearing the smoke to reveal a miracle: the cake resting in Lola's mitted hands.

"I was baking for Holly," she explained, setting the cake on the counter. With a rag, she began to mop up, mumbling all the while. She was sorry, she didn't mean to keep me, I could go if I wanted.

I didn't want. Something about her helplessness pulled at me, or maybe it was just the fact that I was early anyway, with nowhere else to go. Plus, with Lola, I got chances to do useful things, like put out fires. Or maybe I was just eager to learn more about this woman, this Lola, about whom—I now remembered—I had dreamed for several nights in a row, dreamed of her complete with her Wellingtons. She had slipped into my inner world without any particular invitation. I planted myself on her kitchen stool.

Her house was built exactly like Holly's, small but high-ceilinged, with the same large central room—Lola had filled it with books, rather than plants—and the kitchen opening onto it, backed by the glass solarium. In the center of living area, a large wooden table stood piled with papers, more books and scrolls in different stages of unfolding. A typewriter crouched in one corner, a tongue of paper caught in the mechanism as if Lola had left off typing at mid-sentence, perhaps distracted by the smell of smoke. As I poked around, Lola explained that the mess was due to her work as an assistant professor at a local college where she taught a general course in the history of religion, as an outgrowth of her specialty, which was prayer in the ancient Near East. She was also an occasional guest in Holly's home, happy to babysit the younger children in a pinch.

As Lola cleaned up, she told me a story about an obscure Victorian named George Smith.

"He taught himself cuneiform on his lunch breaks when he wasn't working a letterpress in Paternoster Row. One afternoon in 1872 he was going through a cache of tablets at the British Museum when he realized that he was reading about a flood. There was a boat caught on a mountain. Doves."

"Ah," I marveled, catching her gaze and holding it, allowing her to expand into the space I was creating for her in my mind. I admit, this is a trick. But she had already colonized my dreams, and she could not have been unaware of the hypnotic effect of her own low voice, so different from Annie's yawps.

"The inscription dated from almost a thousand years before the earliest account of the Flood." Her hands moved gracefully as she talked, like the doves she'd mentioned. "That's what got me into this business—that story."

She pulled off her sweater. Beneath, she was wearing a thin t-shirt, no bra. The armpits of her t-shirt were dark. With a toothpick, she poked the cake in several places and checked the result for crumbs.

"My new work concerns more recent history," she continued. "Do you know about Amnon of Mainz?"

I shook my head. "Should I?"

"He's associated with a famous prayer. Actually, it's more like a hymn. It's the one you hear at Yom Kippur, about the broken pottery."

"We are as broken pottery," I repeated, astonished to discover the words rising up inside me despite years of conscious atheism. "We are the dream that flies."

"Exactly." Just visible through the solarium's glass wall, a group of geese honked as they flew toward the house in formation. "Tradition claims Amnon as the prayer's author. But there's no proof. All we have is a report from two centuries later, when a twelfth-century rabbi, Isaac ben Moses of Vienna, claimed the story came to *him* in a dream. In which the prayer came to Amnon when his persecutors cut off his hands and feet, after he refused to abjure his faith. It was a terrible story." She glanced at me in the appraising way that my patients sometimes did when they told awful secrets, checking to see that the revelation had not blown me away as they had been annihilated themselves.

"He was tortured."

"Yes. Or at least, that is the legend."

"Go on," I said, struggling to keep Amnon distinct from Holly in my mind. This was my job, in those days—to stay present while another person unwound the gauze from a festering interior wound. All my training was oriented toward reversing the ordinary reaction, to turn toward these things rather than away from them. I was still working on it.

"When did the story originate?"

"Ninth century. But a version of it was recently discovered in a cache of documents in Old Cairo. The cache is even older."

Lola's historical perspective calmed me, as did the homely cake steaming on the counter. I suppose that's just what happens when myth falls into history—it domesticates, it modulates. It grows up. Lola slipped her mittens on again and overturned the pan on a rack. The cake slipped free but before it could settle, she'd flipped it again, so it landed properly, bottom-down. Kitchen magic—a subject best avoided, given my present vulnerability. With Annie gone for weeks, I had only my unpatterned nights, which contained no accounting, no girl by the gooseneck lamp, and certainly no baked goods.

"The idea of dust to dust isn't new," she continued, brushing crumbs from the plate's edge. One landed on my lap. I picked it up, tasted it: vanilla, egg, something faintly floral. Lola went on: "We have it from Ecclesiastes. But the specifics of the prayer matter a lot more. Like, *we are as broken pottery*. That's not metaphorical. That's real. Broken pots are all over the ancient world."

"Ostraka," I said, another word that bubbled up from nowhere.

She laughed, delighted. "So you *know*."

It was a seduction, of course; she was lonely, looking for understanding and companionship. She smiled again, shyly, and I squeezed her hand, letting her know this was not a classroom, and I was not a bored student. She returned the pressure, working the palm of my hand like she would work anything else that arrived in her life tightly rolled and bound, unfolding me one layer at a time.

My mouth was dry. I swallowed, wanting more than anything not to blow this moment, and knowing, in my usual abstracted way, that my insufficiently-analyzed self-disgust would make me likely to do just that.

"Honestly, I have no idea what I'm doing." She backed off, sensing my hesitation. But an ashy smudge on her chin drew me toward her, an imperfection made irresistible by its smallness, which meant even I could rectify it, and I did, with one swift motion of my hand. The dust of ages clung to her hair; she smelled of cake; I sucked her fingers and grit cracked between my teeth.

By spring I was spending most nights at Lola's. She would work and bake into the wee hours, even as I slept, lulled by her noises—the clack of her typewriter, the whirr of her hand mixer, the muffled *whumpf!* of the gas oven coming on. In the morning, I'd find a pile of fresh typescript alongside a zucchini bread, a basket of corn muffins, a pile of cinnamon twists. Lola leaned against the counter, sipping coffee in her spattered bathrobe as she paged through some forbiddingly titled and extensively footnoted scholarly journal.

"Sleep is your friend," I would tell her, around a big, sweet bite of her baking.

"Not *my* friend," she would reply, and set the percolator going again. Usually, it would be around five in the morning. I wouldn't have to be at the hospital until nine, so I would return to our bed, which smelled of sex, tangy and familiar, and fall asleep pleased that this bothered me much less than it used to.

Later, I would offer Lola sleeping drugs—not a prescription, which would be too unethical even for me, but samples

I took home from work because they were overwhelming the clinic's cupboards anyway. Though Lola accepted the pills, she neither took them nor spoke with me about not doing so. Perhaps I'd crossed a line—one of the tricky ones whose breach is not significant enough to merit further discussion, though it should. I found the pills in odd nooks later, when hunting for other things—floss, extra batteries, a paper clip. One packet, with single capsule gone, had been thrust into the nightstand drawer where we kept the rubbers. Perhaps I should have made more of this discovery. I did note it. But discreet politesse again held sway, and besides, my days were too full already. Holly took every free thought I had. Well, not every free thought: My baker-scholar occupied a few thoughts, too. Coming from the hospital, I often stopped at the grocer's for butter and sugar, things Lola needed. As I drove, I watched the sky for birds, smoke, anything. Signs.

SIX WEEKS INTO OUR at-home sessions, Holly's hearing deteriorated, and her speech grew strange. She stopped speaking, like a radio signal cutting out. Juliet feared Holly would despair. But Holly, resourceful Holly, who had learned sign language during her only year at college, simply switched channels, from speech to gesture—and writing. She signed everything she could; what she couldn't, she wrote on slips of paper, napkins and receipts, whatever was to hand.

We were in session as usual, and she was pointing to a glossy large-format *National Geographic* that lay open on the coffee table to a feature article titled "The Last of the Nuba," as photographed by some celebrity shutterbug whose name I no longer recall. The photographs were intimate, as if taken with a zoom lens trained on people unknowingly going about their daily business in a hot climate that kept them mostly naked, while their remoteness kept them innocent both of their nakedness and whatever meaning it might have to onlookers. A teenage girl, who was not dressed but only jeweled, commanded my attention. As the photographer surely intended, I was drawn to the innocent cleft, lightly fuzzed, atop the two strong legs, their litheness accentuated by surface effects, light sliding on oiled skin.

Holly was watching me closely, virtually unable at this point to lift her head.

Here was the healthy body Holly wanted, and it was so far from the degraded one she had.

"Why are you asking me to look at this?" I didn't even try to hide my revulsion.

Aren't they beautiful? she signed.

I wanted to retort: Only if you found exploitation beautiful. But my discomfort was my problem. Holly, who owed me nothing, should not need to make allowances for me.

"Perhaps," I offered, "it is just a matter of taste."

She wrote something down. Still sure I found her repugnant—my prissy response probably didn't help in this regard—she was careful to let go as soon as she felt me take the slip of paper. *The composition*, she'd written.

I thought: And you, decomposing. Like Amnon of Mainz. And, like him, offering up your agony on scraps of paper. In Cairo, a thousand years ago, these fragments would be saved, to be re-found, years later, by a knock-kneed woman who came to me in dreams wearing yellow rubber boots. That day, when our session ended, I abandoned Holly to a room full of paper slips. One of the children, or more likely, Juliet, would have to collect them. Did Juliet read the scraps? Did she talk with Holly about what was on them? I hoped so; I trusted Juliet to do what I could not, to hold Holly through whatever she could not express: shame, desire.

Driving back, I struggled to breathe. The panic grew so bad I had to pull over, just outside the Potomac park entrance, between the river and the curved flower beds. I rested my head on the wheel, unable to rid myself of an image of Holly's body superimposed on the *National Geographic* photographs.

I exhaled shallowly into my cupped hands. Where had this image come from? Could Holly possibly *want* me? Once raised, this question was hard to bear, especially since I was staying almost every night just across the road with Lola. No one could miss my car parked in her driveway. Was that my job—to teach Holly, who had already been denied so much, about not-having?

It seemed cruel.

Then it hit me: Instead of a reasonable regimen of medication, I had offered hypnosis to Holly. And despite the fact that this intervention accomplished precisely nothing, Holly had complied. Suffered. Endured. One thing she did *not* do was complain, because in that case, her mother would have continued to wreak her quiet havoc with the nurses. Which was, in fact, the pain to be addressed. It was all clear now. Unlike me, Holly had known from the start that the pathology I was treating had nothing to do with her. And perhaps my visits did not, either. It was possible that I merely liked her neighborhood—or, more precisely, her neighbor.

It was dusk. Clerks in flannel suits streamed from office buildings. A police cruiser passed without stopping, to my relief. I didn't want to have to explain myself, to insist that I was fine, just a little tired, as you would expect from a doctor coming from work. Downriver choppers churned smoke, spindrift over the freeway. Blinkers blinked. Wipers wiped. On greased rails the year slipped; a cormorant retracted its wings and plummeted; the radio warned of frozen roads. I lifted my head, wanting a better look at the river, those headlights, that smoke.

A freak storm started soon after, the snow falling in wet clumps. The accumulation was so bad that I had to ski to the clinic the following day. Amazing sight: a psychiatrist pumping down a snowy city street on cross-country skis. Too bad there was no one to see it: The buildings were all shuttered, and even the clinic was deserted, though I had the radio for company. According to the announcer, the smoke plume I'd seen the day before was the last worldly residue of a young man who had set himself on fire in the park, protesting something or other. All day, alone in the clinic, I could not get the picture out of my mind. On some level, I believed the man was me, or should have been, as punishment for what I'd done, or failed to do, with Holly. With Annie. With Lola.

Whom I phoned in desperation. No doubt she heard it in my voice. She agreed to stay at my place the following night, after my shift ended. The streets were clear by this time but I had to ski home anyway, as there was no other place to store my skis. By the time I reached my apartment, my prescription pads had nearly frozen in my pockets. Lola removed them, flipping the pages as if to assess some obscure damage, and stacked them on the cluttered night table beside an academic paper about a lost Elamite matriarchy written by a woman whose work Lola did not much admire. My rejected gift, the novel by the respectable New Englander, was in there, too, but I was too worn out to note its exact position in the mess.

"What binds Holly to life?" Lola asked me, after I'd poured out the story of my last two days.

"She's *twenty*." The question seemed incredible. "*Life* binds her to life."

"You mean the future she doesn't have anymore. To which she felt entitled." Lola frowned. "I guess everyone feels that way." Her exhaustion told on her face, a dulling film that reached even to her eyes. "Just as it was five thousand years ago," she said, and gestured toward the monograph on the night-table. "And will be, I suppose, for another five thousand."

"At least," I said sourly, and turned out the light.

Where Holly's cherub face was unlined, Lola's, in the near-dark, bore marks of her advancing maturity, fine lines that would eventually become furrows, the dermatology that resulted from a decade spent hunched over manuscripts. She rubbed her face as if to erase what I had just noticed.

"Lola," I pleaded, afraid my scrutiny had discomfited her. "Tell me again, about Amnon of Mainz."

"You always want a bedtime story." Her tolerant smile did not quite conceal her frustration. Where guessing at the contents of other people's heads was for me a confusing and often dicey professional skill, for Lola the same work was a straightforward matter of analysis, according to a procedure that had been laid down well in advance. With hermeneutics on her side, she was free to act as though such risks did not exist, as if everything short of mortality could be reversed, undone, by the close and exact attention demanded by scholarship, the tranquilizing apparatus of *loc. cit.*, *et al.* Still, her work was a far cry from Annie's faith in cost analysis and demography, which had come to seem limited, unimaginative, falsely reassuring. Or maybe it just comes down to this: Lola believed in interpretation, whereas Annie preferred to stick to the facts. And, *mirabile dictu*, I'd finally taken a side.

Or so it seemed to me then. Looking back, it is hard to know.

From one of my thawing prescription pads on the nightstand Lola tore a page and scrawled on it.

"Look," she said, and show me an inverted triangle with a fourth line, like a gash, that stretched upward from the vertex. "Bet you can't guess what it is."

"I do believe that is a dirty picture," I said.
I didn't say: But not as dirty as *The Last of the Nuba.*
She pinched my arm.

"It's the sign for woman, you prude. In cuneiform."

I stared. The vertices might be the women in my life: Holly, Lola, Annie. Perhaps such things just came in threes, like bad luck, or the Fates. Or perhaps the inscription was itself the important element, a symbol of our exigent need to relieve ourselves of whatever presses on the mind.

"How old is it?"

"The earliest cuneiform inscriptions date from about 3000 BC."

"Your point?"

"It seems we have known something about this for a long time."

"The triangle," I said. My mind swarmed, as if suddenly filled with locust-like supervisors ready to pounce on my incorrect answers. "Was it three *separate* strokes?"

"I don't think so. A wedge pressed into the wet clay—"

"And then the insertion," I blurted.

Lola smiled patronizingly, and at that moment I despised her. There was so much I didn't know, and would not soon—or, possibly, ever. Headlights from a passing car lit the room briefly and dissipated, like the skeptical light in Lola's eyes. The car turned the corner with a screech that threatened to haunt me forever. *Interpret,* I ordered myself, as if the truth might yet set me free.

And there it was, the truth: Annie had needed to push me away, and perversely, the rejection made me try even harder. With Lola, though, the question never came up. How could it? We'd emerge panting from the twisted sheets, so startled to discover ourselves in separate skins that speech, that earliest achievement after walking, would be impossible for hours.

One afternoon Holly was trying to teach me to spell her name. She had been for some time teaching me to sign, a few minutes at the end of each session. I'd permitted this, thinking it would help us communicate but with the deeper intention (it seems clearer in retrospect) of suggesting that our conversations would continue somehow, after her death, in the memory of the impressions we made on each other, when we touched.

She covered my hand with her own, pressed where I'd screwed up. I signed back, trying to be more precise, more articulate. My tendons ached. We'd been at it a while. What life is: aching effort. Trying, in every sense. She took her hand away. We went on like this, haltingly, week after week. Meanwhile, Annie stopped calling, which was fine because her calls tended to upset Lola, who said nothing but cooked with less joy and wrote with less brio whenever Annie was too much on my mind. As it turned out, I missed the cooking and the writing more than I missed Annie and her calculator, and so I let Annie go. The seasons turned; the leaves fell and so, too, the first real snow. Through all of it, my rejected suitor's gift sat on the night table, with the scattered prescription pads and Lola's abandoned monographs. But Lola was still in the bed, and so, seeing no reason to complain, I did not. I'd learned my lesson, even if I still could not say precisely what the lesson was. I continued to visit Holly in the afternoons, when she talked to me in the language of her ideal body, smiling, flirting, shifting the covers to divert my attention to and from aspects of her real body, which underwent increasingly frequent and dismal fallings apart. A run of good days would be interrupted by a decompensation—a loss of feeling in a joint, a numbness that spread from the tip of her nose to her whole face—followed by a period of stability that would in turn be lost. As she taught me to sign simple words like *honey* and *milk*, I associated the gestures with the feel of her hands, the occasional touch of a forearm, smooth and cool and, above all, so young.

The night we celebrated Lola's thirtieth birthday was bittersweet; I had not yet proposed and didn't intend to. Not after Annie. Still, Lola didn't leave. I wondered how long she could hold out, how long I could. My neurosis, if that's what it was, generalized until I could no longer trust myself with patients. I found a position in government-sponsored research. I still worried about marriage, but I tried to do so in an ordinary way, by finding an older mentor like any other ambitious young man with his future much on his mind. My new supervisor, a ruddy-cheeked former manufacturing executive who had not a single insect-like quality, fit the bill well enough, and with him I wondered if perhaps that was what marriage was like, a marathon of withholding. He replied, straightforwardly, that it was. He was unequivocal on the point—but he was unequivocal on most things.

Holly was dying then. A whistling melancholy eddied around me, especially in the car park near my office, as I thumped up and down the dingy stairwell, meeting no one, no one meeting me. I took comfort from a set of new clothes, blue jeans and boots, the uniform of people who were *relevant*, to misuse one of Annie's words. She meant people who had quotable opinions on current events, but I preferred to think of relevance in terms of labor with things you could see and touch. "You're romanticizing," Lola observed with an ironic smile—for she was rather romantically aproned herself, kneading a loaf of wheat bread in her kitchen as she spoke—but she wasn't wrong, either. Maybe I simply needed something to idealize. I wept through the Holy Days, and grew hysterical, if that is the word for it, at the recitation of the Unetaneh Tokef: *We are as broken pottery. We are the dream that flies.*

Holly passed away after Thanksgiving, in the last lowering days of November. Nothing happened, except that one afternoon, a dead leaf fluttered in the periphery of my vision. I turned to see the leaf burn up, and I heard a cry that was like a sheet of foil tearing. That was all: a little leaf disintegrated with a cry. I got the call a few hours later. It was her father, slurring drunk, but by then I too was numb, having used the time to anesthetize myself by laboring over the preparation of a few words, mainly of gratitude for the chance to treat Holly, and admiration for her and for this man and his wife. I remember saying something shamefully intellectualized about their fine parenting. Her father rang off, no word of thanks or anything else either, apart from a rough-voiced goodbye. I suppose I deserved it. But there it is again, the cry of ripping tin, the hiss of a leaf going to ash.

After the funeral, Holly's family gathered at the house. Lola was there, with one of her cakes. Juliet wandered, dazed, through the downstairs rooms. In the kitchen, where even the linoleum seemed hard and echoic as marble, I drained my coffee and refused a refill. Lola and I left together, buttoned into our coats. As we made our way down the walk, Lola looped her arm through mine, and in the moment before I recoiled, I knew just how it felt to belong.

Dance Hall Days

Although family therapy consumed more time than basketball practice and did not at all improve my odds of attending my first-choice college, I had no choice about going. My sister's suicide attempt had alarmed my parents, and they were taking every precaution against relapse.

Horse, meet barn door. Bird, meet coop. I am trying to say: It was all so predictable.

Before our first session, my mother and I piled into my father's hatchback and off we went to Lesser Memorial, where Zenobia was shut up in the adolescent ward. The receptionist directed us to an outbuilding at the edge of the grounds where our assigned therapist was waiting. I followed my parents down a path alongside the main building and across a meadow ringed with tall pines. It was the first real day of spring, warm enough to be uncomfortable.

The therapist's office was stifling, but the therapist—a slim brunette in dun-colored separates—looked completely at ease, tucked like a wren into a big office chair. Margaret introduced herself, apologized for the lack of air conditioning, and invited us to sit. We arranged ourselves on the sofa, perspiring meekly. Zenobia arrived, squired by a thickset orderly in scrubs who, before leaving, slotted a file folder—her medical record, I guessed—into a clear plastic box on the wall. Zenobia looked like a washed-out version of herself—no makeup, lank hair, visible roots. A pink plastic hospital bracelet circled her wrist.

Until this moment my sister and I had shared everything, from toys and clothes to the scant attention of our parents. Even our mother did not refer to us individually but only as a hyphenated compound: Zinn-and-Zeno. But now Zenobia had things of her own—a medical record, a hospital bracelet, an identity as a certified psychiatric in-patient. Whereas the only trace I'd leave would be a damp impress on Margaret's sofa—shameful but deniable, unofficial. Well, there were many differences between me and Zenobia, despite how interchangeably our parents treated us. How everyone treated us.

Everyone, that is, except for Margaret, who saw the problem right away and was always careful to point out differences, making me more aware of them as well.

This was good for me, but it wasn't always comfortable.

We met this way for several weeks, perhaps two months. Margaret chirped repeatedly that *what happens in this room, stays in this room*, but the reality was not even close. I developed a habit of shoving my fingers between the sofa cushion and the frame, and as a result I often left with odd items: a stray pill, a nickel. There were other exports, less literal. After sessions ended, we escorted Zenobia back to the main building, deposited her on the ward, and hightailed it to the parking lot where my father started the car while my mother reapplied her lipstick. That summer she favored pale neutrals, sandy colors with names like Life's a Beach. She twirled the lipstick back down the tube, smacked her lips, checked the mirror one last time, and then the fighting began.

They left me out of it, but overhearing them rehash the session, apportioning blame for every thought and feeling, spoken and not, was still unpleasant. I didn't like playing spectator to what should have been strictly their sport. Soon I was taking the bus home in order to give my parents time to expend their strange energies. To cool off, was how I thought of it, though there was never anything cool between them, not at all.

Toward the end of our therapy summer, I scored a ticket to a Wang Chung concert. It was on a Friday night, after one of our therapy sessions. The ticket made me feel odd, as if I were about to shirk an important responsibility. On the day of the concert, we finished up with Margaret and my parents bickered all the way back to the parking lot. I was sixteen years old, sitting at a bus stop outside a mental hospital, and the tablet I'd found in the crack in Margaret's sofa had just pitched me into low orbit. Fluff bloomed between my ears. I stuck my dandelion head between my knees, taking shallow breaths so as not to blow myself away.

OUR FAMILY'S LARGER PROBLEM had something to do with resemblances, a generalized failure to discern between things and people who were similar but not identical. The day of the concert, after Margaret had closed the session with one of her homilies about how I was *this* and Zenobia was *that*, I was no longer in the mood to see Wang Chung. More precisely, I no longer resembled the person who had made those plans. What I did feel was tired—of homework, school days, laundry, grocery shopping, family therapy, Zenobia and her drama. Above all, I was tired of hearing all the ways in which I was or was not *just like* my sister.

Here is a fact beyond resemblances: Wang Chung came to Providence the year after the death of Papa Frank, my mother's father. I still missed his voice, the way he announced his arrival in our breezeway singing:

Daisy, Daisy, give me your answer, do!
For I'm half-cray-zee, all for the love of you!

My mother mourned the loss in her way. Where she was previously neat, she now scattered her things all over the house—shoes, glasses of water, cups of tea. She buried household items in the yard: silver spoons, curtain tie-backs. Her wedding ring disappeared; I suspect she buried that, too. After rain, the objects glinted under hedges and in the moist, dark gap the yard guys always left between the lawn and the driveway. She also enforced new dietary restrictions. For instance: It was very important that my food choices did not resemble hers in any way. For weeks after Papa Frank died, my mother prohibited me from eating white foods—bread, pasta, milk, vanilla ice cream, all forbidden—while she ate only cottage cheese and Epsom salts. She needed white things, she said, because if she didn't limit her diet in this way, she would die, too.

"A diet to die for," she called it, "and no dyes, either. Nod yes, Zinnia, so I know you're listening."

Instead of white food—or non-food, in the case of the Epsom salts—I ate only red apples, out of spite. I favored the big waxy ones with ivory flesh and thick skin the color of a beating heart.

"Don't be difficult," my mother advised me, after I'd piled my apple cores on the coffee table.

I didn't know any other way to be.

Home, home on the range, I sang in my mind, another of Papa Frank's greatest hits. *Where the deer and the antelope play—*

During the weeks I bickered with my mother over food, Zenobia ate everything she could stick in her face. Red, white—it made no difference. After some months of this, my mother duly informed Zenobia, for her own good, that she was a fatty.

Zenobia was actually normal-sized, just bloated from all the eating. Plus, because of Papa Frank, her face was often contorted and shiny with snot and tears. My mother's problem was not with Zenobia's weight but with her very being, as a child who still had a live father and the luxury of mourning her mother's dead one.

And so it happened that Zenobia, who knew her own flaws as well as anyone, looped some twine around her neck and suspended herself from the curtain rod alongside the brand-new curtains from Laura Ashley.

Like I said, Zenobia wasn't fat—but she was definitely too heavy for this maneuver. The rail broke. Zenobia crashed. My father thundered down the hallway; my mother followed, her heels loud on the hardwood.

Zenobia's door hit the adjacent wall. In my bedroom, I froze.

"JESUS. CHRIST."

Since then I haven't been able to stop playing the scene in my mind. Zenobia must have been on the floor, her eyes glassy, her neck bruised, her face wet with the usual snot and tears.

The house became completely silent.

In this interval of quiet Dr. Teller was called. An emergency meeting was arranged. Dr. Teller met us at Lesser's intake pavilion, a cold atrium with white Naugahye sofas and an Astroturf-colored carpet. He was wearing a jacket and tie even though it was eleven at night. He took one look at the four of us—my red-faced father, my ashen mother, black-and-blue Zenobia, and oblivious me stretched on a white sofa, nibbling a Red Delicious while admiring my reflection in the night-darkened glass—and admitted Zenobia on the spot.

ONE DAY WHEN MY mother and I were visiting Zenobia, Dr. Teller came onto the ward. A group of patients—all female—buzzed around him, and he smiled as if he had no idea what the fuss was about. I caught him looking me up and down, in the way that a doctor isn't supposed to. I smiled, and two pink rosettes appeared on his cheeks. He stuck his nose into a chart.

My mother cried: "How *love* blooms!"

"Like a battered fucking onion," I said.

"Language!" barked the ward nurse. Only the girl with Tourette's was allowed to curse, because she didn't have a choice.

"Battered!" my mother repeated. "Have you seen my bruises?"

I had, but because it pained me to acknowledge them, I only said, "You are golden fried."

MY JOKE WAS LOST on my mother, whose singularity of vision precluded much of a sense of humor. That clarity was something I liked about her. But, as I told Dr. Teller, it also got her into trouble.

Take the Khrushchev delusion. Now *that* was a singular vision. When my mother was pregnant with me, she became sure that Nikita Khrushchev was living next door. She also came to believe that she had been divinely selected to bear this man's baby, that is to say, me. My destiny was to blow up the Eastern Seaboard with an atomic bomb made with white beets from White Russia. They were already growing, she said, in the backyard.

She revealed this, I'm told, after Papa Frank busted through a locked door to find me sitting in my crib, navel-deep in the contents of my diaper. Evidently I'd been screaming my head off for some time. Needless to say, imagining herself to be the virgin mother of some Russian Vishnu was not acceptable to anyone, and my mother spent several months on Lesser's locked ward, anticipating Zenobia's visit by a good decade and a half.

"So being here is a kind of homecoming," I told Dr. Teller.

He smiled. He liked wordplay. "But for whom?"

He was also a man who knew when to use *whom*.

I told him what Papa Frank had told my mother: *Your mind plays tricks.*

"Well," responded Dr. Teller. "That is another perspective."

Dr. Teller collected perspectives like Imelda Marcos did shoes. To have a single perspective was impossible as far as he was concerned. He walked this talk by taking both sides of any argument; if there was a third (or fourth, or fifth) side, he'd take each one in turn, just for fun. Which, from another perspective, might be called *showing off*—but I'm probably only saying that out of competitiveness. I wanted a mind of quicksilver, too.

At Lesser, they strapped Mom to a gurney and zapped her head every other day for a month. She didn't remember anything about the shock treatments, except that they gave her headaches. No memory but pain: this, I believe, was the point.

Zenobia was there, too, her hair standing on end as she floated in my mother's womb. A kind of homecoming, as I said. Like Mom, she has no memory of it, either.

"DID YOU HAVE A HAPPY CHILDHOOD?" Dr. Teller wanted to know.

"Of course!" I cried, obscurely offended.

In fact Zenobia and I soaked up malaise like pickles in vinegar. My father subscribed to the 1950s variety of fatherhood: home at five, enraged by six, snoring before the television by seven, and gone in a puff of exhaust at dawn the next day. On weekends he slept. We had to be very quiet, otherwise he would burst out of the bedroom roaring like a poked grizzly bear. No wonder my mother preferred her inner world of international scandals and questionable produce. At least the absurdity amused; my father was cruel, but cruelty is boring, and if you can point that out, you can defeat it. Imagine yawning at the Marquis de Sade's. The whole night would be ruined. Whenever someone asked my mother what my father did for a living, she only shrugged. *He brings home the bacon, I fry it up in the pan.*

When I can, she'd trail off, her eyes blanking ceilingward. *When I can-can-can.*

"You and your vignettes," Dr. Teller complained in his mild way. "Everything you say is so *composed.*"

"Spontaneity's overrated. Not to mention inefficient. Condensation is so *necessary.* I want to be completely transparent with you. But then, if I were totally transparent," I reflected, "that would mean that I was invisible."

"That's like a pun."

"It's like a superpower," I corrected him.

His eyes were kind. His pen was poised. "But were you happy, Zinnia? As a child?"

What did I know of happiness? It's true that I was a good kid, or good enough: I had solid grades and steady friends, I played flute in the marching band, and I made the varsity basketball team in my sophomore year. Limits I mostly observed—speed, curfew, seatbelt. I was upright, breathing, not obviously damaged.

I DIDN'T TOUCH ALCOHOL OR DRUGS, either, but don't let that add any shine to my halo. The truth was, I didn't have those friends, so I never went to those parties. Zenobia was the one who ran with that crowd. Apparently she attended some real ragers in abandoned parking lots and the woods. Who knew?

At the hospital, Zenobia sought advantages to press. When the staff wouldn't let her dye her hair, she persuaded every disaffected kid on the ward—that is to say, all of them—to drape toilet paper over the bare trees in the quad, the raw buds pink against the white paper and the whiter sky. Heads were shaken, meetings were called, a drenching rain resolved the practical problem, and then everyone was on to the next crisis. The following week, Zenobia contrived a romance with another patient, dismaying the staff for other reasons. Once I caught a glimpse of him—bandaged from wrists to elbows, his pale face obscured by a dark mop of headbanger hair. He reminded me of long shots gone bad on the ball court, nothing but air.

Some things I'll never forget about Lesser: the cafeteria's reek, the rosewood banister that hugged the curving central staircase, the dusty rose carpet that went all the way up.

In the afternoon, the nurses brought out medications in little paper cups arrayed on trays like hors d'oeuvres.

"How in the world do they keep them straight?"

"Look around you, dumbass," Zenobia told me. "What makes you think they keep them straight?"

The place did not seem badly run. Certainly it was no worse than our house.

One of Zenobia's new friends, the girl with Tourette's whom—yes—I've already mentioned, was watching me closely. "They FUCK you up," she began, "your mom and dad they FUCK up the meds every SICK BITCH day."

She cursed like my father did, hammering the diphthongs, making me jump.

"EVERY! BITCH! DAY!"

"You know, that reminds me—" I said, trying to sound like I didn't mind, like I was perfectly accustomed to people shouting obscenities for no reason—

"BITCH FUCK! WHOOOO-ERRR!"

"Reminds you of what, Zinnia," my sister asked sweetly.

My chest tightened and I inhaled, desperate to enlarge the space within. "It reminds me—"

"BITCH SICK SLIT SLUT *CUNT*!"

"Never mind," I muttered as that inward space collapsed. "I forgot."

The girl softened. "They do fuck you up," she said, her voice now completely normal. "Before I was omitted, I was homicidal, suicidal—"

"Fratricidal?" offered Zenobia.

They exchanged glances.

"Zenobia," the girl giggled, "you're gonna get *in trouble*—"

Zenobia lit herself a cigarette and offered one to the girl, who took it.

Because I was not offered a cigarette, I said, "Actually Zenobia is too fat to be a *whoo-errr*."

Zenobia, frowning, exhaled. "How small your world is," she told me. "So snug and safe."

"Zinn-and-Zeno!" my mother trilled from the nurse's desk. That day she was dressed in a sleeveless white linen ensemble accessorized with a long strand of pearls. "Family therapy starts in five minutes," she said, adding darkly, "if you can stand it."

A nurse handed the shouting girl another cup with a pill in it.

"Cunt," the girl said matter-of-factly.

The nurse shook her head and walked away.

"You meant it that time," said Zenobia.

"Meaning it, schmeaning it." The girl tipped the cup to her mouth. She was so convincing I almost didn't see her palm the pills.

DR. TELLER AND I WERE now seeing each other in regular one-on-ones. Because my mother had decided that Zenobia was the one who needed help, she refused to drive me to these appointments, so I took the bus. I didn't mind. I liked the bus for its anonymity and the escape it provided from parental supervision. Dr. Teller's office, which overlooked the pine-ringed meadow, was growing on me, too. As was Dr. Teller, if I am honest. His gaze was sharp and clear, his eyes the color of a pool on the first day of summer. I liked the feeling he gave me, as if the world could be a settled place, where a person could breathe without being hassled for needing air.

On those blessed unaccosted bus rides, I liked to imagine Dr. Teller in an evening, tilted in his easy chair, dreaming back the day. *Home, home on the range,* sings my inner Papa Frank. As ever, Dr. Teller leaps up to adjust the light and the air conditioning, just like he does when I am in his office. We settle into each other's company, and in those moments, I become someone else. Someone better. Someone I can't afford to be, not yet. A malleable person, non-difficult. Someone whose sister doesn't hang herself from a curtain rod in order to feel loved.

"What does Zenobia have to do with my opinion of you?" he asked me one afternoon.

Give me your answer, do—

His question struck me silent. We were so close, Zenobia and I, that I simply couldn't parse it. I tried to imagine his perspective: A psychiatrist in early middle age finds himself trying to connect with a teenage girl who sees the world through a split frame cobbled from her own perspective and that of her crazy sister.

"That's a leading question," I said, still being difficult, still committed to that.

When his hair got long, it curled over his collar. He couldn't see it, but I could.

ZENOBIA RETURNED for a few days at midsummer. Her first order of business was to raid my closet. I found my favorite jeans on the floor of her room, torn clear across the knee. What a fucking waste: I'd blown five whole weeks of babysitting money on them.

Zenobia stood in the doorway flicking the overhead light.

"Stop that before I barf on you."

"Bitch, you wouldn't dare."

"You shouldn't take my clothes without asking," I said, hating myself for sounding prissy.

"They were ugly jeans," Zenobia replied. "You're better off."

"But they don't fit you! You have fat knees."

"Cunt," she said thoughtfully, as if understanding something for the first time. "Whore."

That night, she set fire to my jeans in the BBQ pit. I smelled them burning from inside my bedroom where I was finally doing my SAT prep.

Outside the air was full of the smell of lighter fluid, a summer smell; and other smells came on, too, a smell of burnt denim and something creaturely that might have been mine.

I turned around and went right back to my problem set. At least SAT prep was still under my control.

The next day, I asked my father to install a lock on my closet.

"You know she'll just break down the door," he said. "Forget about it."

I owned a pair of black jeans, a black t-shirt, a black sweatshirt, some socks and underwear. From that moment on, that was all I wore. Every night I washed and dried this wardrobe, which consisted of what could only be taken off me by main strength. Sitting atop the dryer, dressed in one of Papa Frank's old shirts, I calculated my grade point average and the days I had left.

"A family is a system," Margaret was saying. "I feel like I can tell you this, Zinnia, because in this system, you're the person who understands things."

I shrugged. I knew the drill. First Mom cried and yelled at Dad, who pretended not to know why she was being so unreasonable. The therapist then solicited feedback from me and Zenobia. I never had a response apart from the unsayable one, that it was all bullshit. Besides, whenever I *had* ventured an opinion, Zenobia made sure no one heard it anyway. So I stayed quiet, and Zenobia ran her mouth the way a biker runs an engine while parked outside the shops on the bougie side of town.

That day, Zenobia described the misery of living with all of us, particularly me. She resented my grades and the awards I'd won, the trophies I'd brought home, and the praise of my teachers.

"What do you think it's like," she wailed, near tears, "to have you for a sister? To have a *perfect* sister?"

"Oh, for God's sake," I snapped. "How would I know?"

I pressed myself into the corner of the sofa and watched the outside world, the slice of it I could see through the window behind Margaret's desk. A breeze lifted the branches of a large Ponderosa pine. Heat shimmered over the parking lot. I stole a glance at my mother. She was staring at Zenobia, holding very still.

"Zinnia," said Margaret. "I feel that you are distancing yourself."

"It's not like I'm so proud of any of the things Zenobia mentioned," I said finally. "I don't even study all that much."

Zenobia wailed, "See what I mean!"

I shrugged. "It's true. I don't."

Margaret stared at me. "You are so brave," she said quietly. "And you," she continued, turning to Zenobia, "are a manipulative bitch."

She hit the diphthong hard. For once I didn't flinch.

Zenobia put her fist right through the wall.

Margaret touched a button on her telephone and an orderly—large, male—appeared in the doorway. A gentle giant, I thought. Then he caught Zenobia in a half-nelson.

My mother cried, "You can't do that!"

"For heaven's sake," my father said cheerfully. He was enjoying this. "Of course he can."

The orderly pulled Zenobia from the room. Zenobia twisted and hissed; she opened her mouth and drooled on his white nursing shoes. "We have to stop," Margaret said. "That's all the time we have for today."

AFTER LEAVING MY PARENTS in the parking lot, I went back in search of Dr. Teller. My head was clear enough; what I needed was to talk. Approaching the double-doors that led to the adolescent ward, I caught sight of him through the glass. I waved and he mimed a punching-out gesture; he was almost off his shift. After a few minutes, he emerged, his eyes narrow slits over shadowed pouches. When we reached the bottom of the stairs, he sank down until he was sitting on the next-to-lowest step. He ran his hand through his hair. He was sinewy under his scrubs, with large hands and feet, and he was about a week from needing a haircut.

"Wanna shoot some hoops, Zinnia? I could stand to move the blood around."

"Sure." Maybe we could talk while we played.

He strode ahead, moving fast. He actually seemed to believe that he could resolve his exhaustion by expending yet more energy. I predicted a short court session.

First thing, he hit a three-pointer. Dumb luck: He had no athletic ability that I could see. I countered with a lay-up, crying FOUL. He cursed, gasping. *Language*, I objected. I must have sounded like the ward nurse. He doubled over laughing, the ball canted off his hip, and, after several deep breaths, gave me the free throw.

I crouched slightly at the free throw line, taking my time. Bouncing the ball, spinning it, letting him catch his breath. I didn't want to win. I just wanted to keep him upright enough to have a respectable outing. "Zenobia put her fist through the wall," I said.

"Why in the world did she do that?"

"You didn't hear?" Bounce, spin, bounce, spin. "Margaret called her a manipulative bitch."

"Margaret?" He guffawed. "And what did she call *you*?"

Bounce, *bounce,* spin. I arced the ball high and straight through the hoop.

"Nice." He caught the ball as it fell. "*What did she call you?*"

"Nothing," I told him. "Nothing but net."

We traded shots for a while, until my shirt was sticking to me and he complained about sweat running into his eyes. A group approached with the physical trainer. They had reserved the court, so we headed for a bench.

"Phew." He mopped his shiny face with his shirt. "Good game."

I took the hand he extended, wanting to be polite, un-difficult. Then the touch became something else. I turned his hand over, traced a line down the center of his palm. He stared at me over his rimless glasses, letting his hand sink into mine. Something was going to happen.

"Yeah, I'm not bad at this." I dropped my hand out from under his and wiped both of mine on my shorts. Was he somehow unaware—of the staff on the court, what people might see? Who was this performance for?

Whom.

"You know, I was supposed to see Wang Chung tonight."

"You don't think you'll make the show?"

"I decided to take the bus home," I said. "And now I'm too late."

"Your problem is not the bus or the clock." He gave me a significant look: Here was an on-ramp if I wanted to take it.

"Right," I told him, all breezy. "My problem is lack of a car."

"Come on," he said, rising. "I'll take you."

HIS CAR WAS FULL of Dunkin Donuts cups, medical journals, and baby stuff—teething rings and pacifiers.

"For your patients?" I asked, plucking a binkie from the ashtray.

"Of course not." He took it from me and dropped it in the pocket of his scrubs. "I have an infant."

Pills on the floor, sample packages. I picked one up. It said: *NOT FOR RETAIL SALE.*

Without taking his eyes off the road, he snatched that away, too.

I recited my address, and we drove for a while. He was not taking the most direct route to my house, and I was not minding the least little bit. Eventually we turned into a parking lot fronting a small beach. A pair of men had planted fishing poles in the sand. The men sat side-by-side on a cooler, holding cans of beer. The bay smelled dead and looked worse, a slick of something oily on the surface. Dr. Teller leaned back, stretching. He smelled like a long day—heat and sweat, cheap disinfectant, cafeteria food.

"Can I ask you something?"

"Sure."

"You see all kinds of crazy. I've been seeing a lot of it, too, lately."

"I bet you have."

"Mom talks to herself in the mirror, she sees things that aren't there, she thinks people are trying to hurt her. But that's all harmless, more or less."

"She's not as sick as some other people."

"She isn't always completely wrong. Zenobia isn't thin. I am—"

"Difficult."

"Not easy."

He turned to me, cocked his head all birdlike. "You don't need your mother to tell you how the world works. Or who you are."

"My mind is stuffed too full of things you want me to keep there," I said. "Advice. Opinions."

"You're right. What I think doesn't matter."

"From your point of view? Or are you telling me about mine?"

He caught my gaze and held it. I stared at my hands, clasped in my lap, one hand holding the other against letting go. Being let go.

All Zenobia had done, probably, was look cross-eyed at my mother.

He was still looking intently at me. If his eyes were a swimming pool, the water was deeper than I thought. Colder, too. Something flashed in his eyes, like a school of fish turning in a shaft of light. His intelligence, I suppose. A creature in the shadows, watching, evaluating.

"Can you drive me home now, please?"

"If that's where you want to go."

The Laundromat

O NCE UPON A TIME, I made a wish, an uncareful wish, in the Harder Laundromat.

I wanted to throw a party for my students. Since September, they'd attended my chemistry tutorial, created to fill an empty afternoon slot while rounding out my practicum year. A party to celebrate the end of all this dullness—school year, tutorial, practicum—seemed like a nice thing. If I privately considered it a celebration of the end of my own training, that was my business. I didn't need to make it about me. But I felt a celebration was in order, and one day I bubbled over, confessing my idea to Lynne.

I've never actually thrown a party, I told her.

Parties aren't hard, she said. Definitely not as hard as chemistry. Tell you what. Next week we'll throw one here at the laundromat. Think of it as a dry run.

I caught our reflection in the plate glass window: two women sitting on plastic lawn chairs, legs crossed left over right, right over left. Behind us, the dryers spun, perfuming the air with fabric softener and scorch.

Let's do it in two weeks, I told Lynne. Maybe you'll forget in the meantime.

Lynne laughed. You chicken.

The next time I visited, I found a sign pinned to the corkboard. Lynne's loopy, sudsy handwriting announced: LET'S PARTY HARDER!

OPEN MIC, the sign continued. OPEN BAR. OPEN HEART. SNAX!

I had been careless, and now I was stuck.

HARDER SITS AT THE CROSS of two roads along a river. When I lived there, the town could still boast an operational woolens mill along with the usual necessaries—church, gas station, pizza parlor, grocery store. The teachers' college, where I was finishing my degree, was an uphill mile from town, not far from the artists' colony. From the spotty clothes spinning in the dryers, you could tell that the artists were mostly painters, though there were others, too: writers, poets.

The laundromat took up the first floor of a narrow two-story house with a steeply pitched roof. A plate glass window gave onto a covered porch with a mild sag. On the roof, a 1950s era sign featured a brunette folding laundry, both the figure and the pile reduced to the minimum number of marks needed to suggest the tableau. During my time in Harder, the porch was always swept neat. Even so, people didn't gather there, perhaps because the building faced west, leaving it in shadow for most of the day.

If the exterior was quiet, the laundromat's interior was loud with weird life. The proprietors left notes around—instructions for emergencies, exhortations to keep the place clean; which people mostly did, though the corners were always a little cobweb-struck. At the high windows in the back, curls of flypaper hung down, heavy with the fat flies that emerged annually in the summer from the attics where they lived all winter long. Beyond the flypaper, people didn't resist them. Exterminations were expensive, and they just came back anyway. To be well and truly rid of them, you had to rebuild your house, which no one had the inclination to do, regardless of the money, which no one had any of either. Houses were passed from parents to children over many generations. The people lived in the houses and their flies lived in the interstices, in attic nooks and behind clapboards. No one liked the flies, but they were inalienable. Harder was a staying place—no exorcisms, no exterminations. Even after I left, something of the place remained with me, a dormant fly in some inner recess.

The first Friday I was alone with Lynne at the laundromat, I stacked my quarters on the washer I preferred, toward the front. Two over, Lynne was frantic, waving an athletic sock. A fly was chasing her.

These damn flies!

She cut in front of me at the soap dispenser.

Hey, I said.

She ignored me.

Shoo! Shoo!

With each "shoo" Lynne dropped another quarter in the slot. She pulled the lever and a box of soap powder tumbled from the machine. She took it and walked off. A fly landed on her head. She ignored that, too.

It was a slim basis for a friendship.

I took a seat near Lynne, who was flipping the pages of *Us Weekly*.

These flies, I said.

You can't have been here long if you're still worried about *them*. Where you from, honey?

I'm getting a master's at the college, I said. In education.

You don't have your own washer-dryer?

Not yet.

I preferred Friday nights for laundry because the laundromat was usually empty. But after that first conversation, Lynne showed up every Friday night. I decided to make the best of it. It wasn't like I had so many friends in Harder.

Lynne, it turned out, was a gas. She dressed young and styled herself "zany" in the way of pretty women who are afraid of seeming cold. She played broad, wiggling her hips while pushing her damp clothes in a rolling cart, taking long strides that were none too steady because, of course, she was wearing stilettos. To a laundromat. On a Friday night. *Zany.* She confided that she was saving up for a Botox shot to erase a tiny line between her eyebrows.

If I don't get it taken care of, she said, I'll have a terrible resting bitch face. I mean, it's already pretty bad. Not that I care. But I'm not *resting*, bitches. I can rest when I'm dead!

BETWEEN TRIPS to the laundromat, I considered the personal details I wanted to share with Lynne. It seemed okay to say that I was a teacher in training, that my position was temporary, just for the year. I didn't mind telling her about my students, how we made volcanoes from vinegar and baking soda, and how, despite the drama of the bubbling lava, the papier-mâché exterior, painted carefully with poster paint, became the locus of the most serious effort. We filled Tupperware containers with homemade slime and observed its behavior on different surfaces—a plastic bag, a window, a kickball. We made experiments with cast-off papers I purchased from a man smoking a cigarette in the front office of a shuttered mill. The office was filled, floor to ceiling, with boxes of overstock, yet he continued to light up. Was he oblivious to the danger? Courting it?

It's a hard town, Lynne intoned. We have in the past hit upon some hard times.

I could only nod. What did I know? Lynne looked at me oddly, as if to remind me of this danger, of my presuming to know. She liked to lord it over me, her status as a native. But since we both knew my presence in Harder was only temporary, and that I would be the one to leave, not her, I let her think what she wanted.

Our Fridays took on heft and definition, like an onion accreting layers underground. Soon we had fellow travelers. One I'll never forget: a girl of late middle-school vintage with brown hair, olive skin, and a dragged-on look. Every week she ran a little pile of black clothing—socks, underwear, one pair of jeans, three black t-shirts, and an oversized sweatshirt that said HARDER—through a machine. She wore pajamas under her big coat. Every week she stayed for two wash cycles, changing into a set of clean clothes in order to wash the pajamas. No mother, I supposed. Or maybe a terrible stepmother. Someone who wouldn't let her use the washer-dryer. The girl seemed so burdened I couldn't even bring myself to ask her name. Maybe that was the right thing to do, to leave her with that much privacy. My own mother had made a bludgeon out of mine, calling *Zinnia, Zinnia,* until I wanted to spit.

As the winter rolled on, Lynne dreamed up schemes and implemented them. A set of steel shelves appeared in front of the plate glass window, each shelf topped with a plank. To this Lynne added an overachieving pothos vine in a chipped pot. Every week she planted two or three smaller pots with its cuttings. She posted help-wanteds on the corkboard and collected half-bags of potting soil, worm casings, extra pots, whatever folks had sitting around. One night, Lynne extracted an S-hook from her purse and dangled it from a strut. It was just the size to hang the watering can that arrived the next day. Someone's dog had chewed it—you could see the bite marks—but it was serviceable. A fire extinguisher appeared next. It was a thoughtful addition. The dryers did tend to get things a little too dry, and it was easy to fail to pay attention.

Lynne posted a notice for a Tuesday night poetry slam, and a bunch of people from the artist colony showed up with poems folded into smudged squares. They stood before the shelves of plants reading to anyone who happened to be there, and made themselves beloved by bringing boxed wine and flasks of Jim Beam that they passed around. One man took a sip and wiped his mouth with the poem he'd just read. I fell in love immediately, though it was the sort of falling that I was used to, a falling that cost me nothing because it was only a sort of theatrical drop from which I knew how to recover, and so it did not vex me.

WITH SO MUCH GOING ON, it seemed that Lynne had forgotten about the party. Then she took me aside and asked me to review her shopping list.

So this is really happening?

You betcha.

I ran my eyes over the list—booze, ice, paper products. Snax?

We'll set out a bag of chips and a big jar of salsa. I must have about ten of them at home. People will bring what they like. There's always too much.

Something slammed into the glass, yawing it, and shot back, leaving behind a web of cracks. At the center of the web was a dark hole where fresh air rushed in with a smell like wet stones.

What the fuck, said Lynne.

In the uncracked portion of the glass, a woman half-hidden by the plants wore a startled look. It took a moment for me to realize that woman was me. A shadow slipped across the street. A pale, feminine face turned toward us, beneath spiky white hair gelled up in a style that was popular decades ago. The light from the laundromat's sign blue-sheened her motorcycle jacket.

I hooked my bag of laundry under one arm and went out. It was a clear night tinseled with stars. On the porch I tripped over an empty can. When I picked it up, it rattled. I peered into the hole, turning the can in the light. Inside were smooth, round river pebbles. The can was dented on one side, where it had hit the window.

I set the can on the porch and swung my foot until it connected, arcing the can into the air. It was a good feeling, making contact. But all the way back to my room, I kept hearing that can. It rattled behind me as I crossed the bridge. As I hurried, so did the can. Turning back, I saw nothing, and nothing again. Yet the sound followed me, and then, as I ran, tilting, around the final corner, that can rattled right across the street.

The next day Lynne texted: Meet me tonight.

I thought: Oh, God.

I texted back: Sure thing. It's towels night anyway.

I'm sorry about this, Lynne said when she arrived, gesturing toward the broken window. She was disheveled, her bare feet stuck into an old pair of sneakers. Shadows darkened the hollows beneath her eyes.

It's my daughter's doing. All she ever wanted was to get the hell out of Harder. Why she's back now, I'll never know. Wish she'd just stay gone.

Lynne muttered about her daughter's situation, legalities that bored and frightened me—case files and hearings, something about the parole board.

Her real name's Mabel, Lynne said, but she changed it at fifteen to Maybelle. This was right after she declared her emancipation. I don't know what she calls herself now. Most of the time she was a shit.

A kid declaring emancipation sounded like bad news. A scene unfolded in my mind: the heavy slam of a front door, a Hefty bag stuffed with clothes and slung over the shoulder, the whiff of burnt plastic as it came toward the face.

So, I said. What about Mabel?

Lynne paused to swallow a mouthful of something invisible and toxic.

Mabel was a hard child, she said. Never met a child so hard. She went looking for her father, that was her first order of business, and she sent a card when she found him. Or thought she did. I don't know the particulars, so I'll just say it did not work out the way she'd hoped. She's twenty-five now, all grown up I expect. Haven't laid eyes on her in almost a decade. Not sure she'd recognize me.

She'd recognize you.

Oh, I don't know. What do I know, though? She was a hard child. One night when she was small I took her outside. It was dusk, early summer, and we'd been in the house all day because she had a fever. But the night was warm and her temp was down so I thought we'd have some fun. Brought two mason jars with lids. Told her we'd catch fireflies.

My plan was to let her run around in the hedges while I did something else. My roses were in full bloom, the first of the season. I wanted to save a few. I heard you could dry them in Epsom salts and that way they would last forever. I filled a shoebox with Epsom salts, set it on the step, and surveyed my roses. Mabel was right beside me, staring.

Mabel, I told her, *take your jar and see if you can catch a firefly.*

She wouldn't move. She just stood there. I tried to show her how to sweep the jar through the dark at the foot of the hedge, where the flies like to be. *Look*, I said. *You just slap the lid on, quick, and see what you can catch—*

There was a firefly right in my jar.

But when I looked up, her hand was in the box, and then it was in her mouth. Sugar, she said, the white grains falling from her hand. You know Epsom salts taste vile, nothing like sugar. I said, *Don't*. But Mabel just kept going. She fisted the stuff into her palm and pressed it to her mouth. Kept staring. Kept chewing.

And now she's back, Lynne said.

Outside, through the big window, the sky was star-scattered, as if Mabel had come back to Harder just to fling that handful of salt into the sky.

When evil shows up in fairy tales it's always moving fast. Usually it's rolling.

I'm pretty sure it was her who broke that window, Lynne said.

The next day the police took their report. Naturally I got a call to come in. The officer was polite enough but there was no mistaking the expectation that I would give my version of events. The conversation was quick. The cop who took my statement didn't take a single note, only twisted her long braid around her finger. I didn't say anything about the can filled with stones. Later I went over the river and back again, wondering if I'd dreamt the whole thing.

THE NIGHT OF THE PARTY, some folks showed up with their dirty clothes. I didn't mind. The whole point of our laundromat interventions was to spin a chore into something less burdensome. Lynne arrived with a dozen bottles of Rolling Rock that she arranged in a washer filled with ice. Folks set six packs and bags of chips on the folding counter. Even the odd little girl was there, pushing quarters into the machines and setting them off so the place was loud with washing. Everywhere I looked, sudsy waves lolled behind the glass windows of the machines. When she got them all going, she smiled at me in a way that seemed at once free and knowing, showing off a chipped front tooth.

Lynne poked my arm. *See?* It's not so hard to throw a party.

Be careful what you wish for. Isn't that what everyone says? What happened next is hard to tell. The lights went out. The front window collapsed. The plant shelves tipped and crashed, and the shattered pots disgorged their contents—a bird's nest fern, a gardenia. Suddenly, the place was blazing. The fire cracked around me. Taking off, I stubbed my toe on something heavy. Someone—I think it was the man with poems in his pockets—found the fire extinguisher and the room disappeared beneath a blanket of foam. Lynne sped out on those heels of hers, shouting her daughter's name.

Jackals

Isn't that lyndon johnson?

Spine arched, head thrown back, Mindy gestured toward the clutch of ex-presidents who'd been figured like saints on a bank of stained-glass windows. Her bracelets glinted; the choker at her neck suggested other possibilities. Mindy was an ostentatious fake and, as usual, Simon wanted to wallop her. But they'd been married so long he'd grown used to such urges and the mechanics of their suppression. Everyone else—they were six that evening, including himself and Mindy—offered bland smiles. They, too, had resigned themselves to Mindy.

I'll be *damned*, she continued, squinting at the windows across the bar, oblivious to Simon's irritation, to the condescension of the group. It *is* Lyndon Johnson.

Yes, someone said, in a dull, down-regulating tone. Right there next to him is Tricky Dick.

Simon tilted his head, hoping this shift in his literal perspective would effect a similar shift on the level of metaphor, permitting him to see his wife differently. Perhaps reality was no more solid than the view through a kaleidoscope, bits of colored glass that could be rearranged with a twist of the mechanism. Twist: Surely Mindy was too old to play the dimwit. Twist: Surely they'd been married too long for that. And yet, there it was: the coquettishness, which hadn't suited her when she was younger and didn't suit her now. But you couldn't change the raw materials; light comes through glass in only one way. That's what he'd been told in counseling. He'd bridled at the advice, but then he was just like that, a man who bridled at advice. Bridling didn't make the advice less apt. It didn't change the reality: she wasn't part of their group. She hadn't gone to school with them; she didn't get their jokes. Maybe he shouldn't have dragged her along.

But then how long had it been since they'd gathered like this? Thirty years? Thirty-five? Simon couldn't bring himself to do the math. Calculation taxed him more than reminiscence as he turned the far corner on middle age. They'd met as first-year psychiatric residents, anxious to shine—and they had, briefly. But time had dulled them all. Jack Stolz had developed the drinking problem they'd all foreseen; Rory Beck had lost all his hair, and much of his vitality, to chemo; and Simon winced when he noticed Kath, with whom he still shared an office, talking around nouns she kept losing. Even King Smalls, who had been such a dynamo, organizing double dates and tailgate parties when the rest of them could scarcely stand from exhaustion, had retired to Florida. How could aging, a natural process, produce so much that felt unnatural? Still it was good to meet, especially here, where time had stopped with Watergate: the chairs and tables were the same, as were the too bright light fixtures that lent the place the familiar if unlovely air of a hospital cafeteria, and then there were the ex-presidents, caught forever in the glass wall of shame.

Rory had extracted a passel of school photographs from his wallet and the pictures were now making the rounds. The grandkids endeared with their cowlicks and gap-toothed smiles, their attention seemingly caught by something exciting just over the viewer's right shoulder. Perhaps it was the prospect of adulthood. It always looked so compelling at that age, Simon remembered. He smiled wider with each photo, aware of making an effort. The others also seemed uncomfortable, their praise coughed up, obligatory. Simon's face ached from all the politesse.

I can't believe, Kath was saying, how much this place has changed. The milk stout isn't even on the menu anymore.

Behind her, a large-screen television was tuned to some athletic contest. Simon could see green fields, and men running across them, and, now and then, a flicker as the signal weakened.

There's a lot that's not on the menu anymore, King was saying. Eggs, steak, butter.

Rory lamented: ice cream! They all winced and then simultaneously burst out laughing. Togetherness had its pleasures. It felt good to share a concern, even if it was only about cholesterol.

Even we aren't on the menu anymore, Kath said.

Her remark brought the usual silence thumping down. Why always this modesty around the topic of sex? Mindy sniffed, and Simon braced himself against another wave of irritation. He would have to try not to find some trivial pretext on which to berate her afterward, in the hotel room.

Kath excused herself with a wave of her clutch.

Speaking of sex, Stolz began, shifting into the chair that Kath had vacated.

Or not speaking, Mindy murmured.

Everyone ignored her—freely since, now that Kath had gone, there was less need to keep up appearances with the opposite sex. Simon felt marginally better: their sexism, at least, remained lively. Though they'd finished school during a period of expanding egalitarianism, he considered them all men of the college in the old style—well, except for Kath, who was not a man at all, of course. She'd been part of the first co-ed housing experiment, when the boys made a point of pissing against her door. The egalitarian movement had assimilated everything, even the pools of piss, and look what had happened: the college didn't produce men anymore, just wave after wave of undifferentiated graduates. You had to be an imbecile not to feel the loss.

Simon's thoughts had only grown less shareable—that was another problem with aging.

Have I got a story for you, Stolz said.

Over Stolz's shoulder, a penalty flag unfurled against the green.

You know what the dementia did to Stanley, Stolz said. His wife had to put him in a home.

Stanley was their teacher, the one they'd all sucked up to, elbowing one another aside in their compulsion to impress. Stolz leaned forward, warming to his story. What a putz. Resentment surged through Simon.

I went to see him, Stolz said. He greeted me same as ever. He was wearing his smoking jacket, looked like he was just on his way to the office. Can you imagine. He sits me down. He looks me in the eye. He says, the women here.

The women! exclaimed King.

Always the women, Rory echoed.

All crazy! Stolz was shouting. Crazy!

Simon said, Yeah?

I mean, Stolz emended, that's what he says to *me*. He says, there's this woman, this—

Old lady?

Mindy touched the tip of her nose, their secret signal: shut up.

I didn't want to actually *use* those words, Stolz backtracked.

Quietly King asked, Where's Kath?

I mean, there's this old *widow*—

Gesticulating, Stolz knocked his glass to the floor.

A flurry of napkins descended, and a round-cheeked girl whom Simon thought too pretty for her nerd glasses swept the shards into a dustpan, the crack of her ass just visible above her belt.

That *is* him, isn't it, Mindy asked, plucking his sleeve. Isn't that LBJ?

Simon didn't respond. It was important to let reality hit people. Stolz, for one, needed a wake-up call. He was obviously impaired.

The waitress returned with a refill.

On the house, she said, handing it to Stolz.

What's this, a sippy cup?

That might actually be appropriate, Simon said.

The waitress made excuses: it had been such a busy night, they'd run out of pint glasses and had to switch to Solos. She eyed Stolz and he stared back mildly—Simon recognized the trick—until she looked away.

Mindy prompted: You were saying, Jack? About the widow?

Mindy would grease the rails of his own oblivion with the same competent charm—for which, it occurred to Simon, he might well be grateful.

Wet-lipped, Stolz was winding up to his punchline: So she'd come into the room, the widow. She was talking a blue streak, the way they do. Stanley listened for a while. And guess what he said?

Just back from the bathroom and trailing perfume, Kath asked: What?

We have to stop.

A shrink's line. Their laughter was polite, indulgent. The curmudgeon would never change. That was the point. They liked to believe that they were similarly faithful to themselves. That their lives expressed an essence that, whatever it might have been, was unquestionably theirs.

Stolz, meanwhile, was staring into his beer. A qualified victory had never been enough for him. Simon remembered a lesson from Stanley: People are like stuck compasses, they don't shift more than five degrees to either side. It was important to keep expectations realistic.

The waitress dropped the check, which was fine by Simon, who had already resigned himself to an early night. Even in residency, their outings often did end this way, with one dumb move that scattered the group. After a scramble for coats, they tumbled onto the street. *Yahtzee!* Mindy sneered behind her hand. The darkness pitched around them and they slipped the mooring their assembly had provided, bidding each other good night.

ON MONDAY, KATH FOUND Simon's door open by a finger's width and the whole office charged with a strange atmosphere. Fraught. Some days, her patients told her, it's better to stay in bed, and she saw the rightness of that view even as she tried to convince them otherwise. Depression had a pedagogy. For one thing, it taught self-preservation. Nothing bad could happen to you if you didn't leave your bed. That self-preservation was more necessary in some contexts than others—well, teaching that was *her* bailiwick.

Most days she felt up to it. Not today. She slipped off her clogs—she preferred to work in socks—and padded to the kitchen where she located her mug, its interior glaze addled with cracks from the stream of hot drinks that lubricated her day. She ran hot water from the dispenser into her cup, dunked a teabag, and, having girded herself with this ritual, went to look in on Simon.

He didn't answer her knock. She considered calling out but then retreated to the kitchen, trying not to feel slighted by his lack of response. A tiny practice like theirs depended on the willingness of each partner to understand the other, to provide quick bursts of support. All she'd done was the professional thing, making sure to check in with him when he seemed to be having a rough time. She didn't deserve the cold shoulder, but then, if Simon was difficult, well, he was just being Simon. She opened a cabinet and became so absorbed in rummaging for a snack that she didn't hear Simon enter the kitchen.

There was a thing, he said, causing her to jump. Sorry.

That's all right.

Like a child taught to watch his step, he'd learned the trick of moving noiselessly. She found a bag of pretzels and slid it toward him, the rigid plastic bag crackling. She wanted him to know she wasn't mad about him creeping up on her, pouncing.

So there was a thing?

The other night at the bar. When you left to use the bathroom.

Oh?

He told her what Stolz had said about Stanley and the older woman who'd accosted him at the home and, in doing so, brought Stanley back to himself, to Stolz, to the world.

That's how Simon made it sound: like the old woman had accosted Stanley.

Oh, that Stanley, she mused, trying to buy time. It was hard to square Simon's sour narrative with what she remembered of that night, its density of shared experience, especially toward the end. Her next words bolted from her: The grand old man can't also be a dirty one, can he?

Who said anything about *that*?

Sorry, she said. How could she have failed to corral that thought? He didn't reply, and she felt even worse. She watched him leave. She knew this aspect of Simon well enough. Beneath the posturing was a core orientation, a way of being in the world that was as much his own as his fingerprints, yet she knew that this quickness to take offence was more obvious to others than it would ever be to himself. To himself he was just *right*.

She'd puzzled over it many times: Who was Simon in that self-righteous moment, and who did she, Kath, become for him? But even after all the cogitating she had to admit that she had no idea. At the bottom lurked an energy she associated to sex. They listened for a living. But for him it was different, Kath thought. For him listening felt like a shock to the body's integrity, like diving into the ocean, enduring that assault on all the senses, one's perception suddenly reduced to green, cold, salt, wet—oh, and the smell, that faintly menstrual rot. He had to stand firm against that, perhaps.

Or else what she felt must be wrong, an echo of her own damage, nothing to do with him at all.

Maybe he was just blurting.

She had an adolescent patient whose eyes were like her husband's. On bad days, she sat with this young woman and failed to listen, distracted by private wonderings: What other children might her husband have? What lies secured her happiness?

She caught Simon in the corridor on his way to lunch.

What did your wife say about Stolz's story?

Simon shrugged, avoiding her eyes. The downstairs door slammed. Her next patient would arrive in moments.

You didn't ask?

What does it matter? She's not one of us.

In her office, Kath located the small compact she kept in her desk and checked her teeth. Pressing her tongue against her lower incisors, she felt for the gunk where she knew it built up. She'd have to see the dentist soon.

Not like us, she thought. What a thing to say.

But then again, what *couldn't* you say after thirty years of marriage?

KATH KNEW SHE WAS TOO wound up to drive. The trip was a mistake, the day too bright, the business ahead—just grocery shopping, which shouldn't have bothered her—overwhelming. Behind her eyes a pressure had built, the tension of psychic material badly repressed. All she wanted was to sit in a darkened room and hold her head. Still the groceries had to be collected. Besides, she pep-talked herself, wasn't she used to doing things on her own, through any sort of madness?

She drove carefully, avoiding potholes.

It was only after she'd parked that she discovered she'd forgotten her list. She donned sunglasses and fussed with her wallet, arranging bills and receipts, waiting for a solution to occur to her. None did. She'd have to work from memory. The pressure behind her eyes intensified.

The store was crowded. She kept her sunglasses on, knowing she looked crazy. So what. She hefted bunches of bananas, heavy yellow-fingered hands. She wished she were wearing headphones.

It was useful to divide problems into types. There were abstract problems, like trying to draw a line between one country and another, and concrete ones, like ordering a milk stout. Similarly, there were thinking problems and feeling problems. Today's problem *felt* like a *thinking* problem, which made it something of a conundrum. She couldn't stop *thinking* about Simon's story, and this inability *felt* bad. Unless it was the story itself that was the cause of the bad feeling, and her rumination was just a symptom. A story could infect you like a virus. Perhaps Stolz's story had made Simon sick in just that way and Simon needed to relieve himself of whatever the story had produced in him, some unbearable state of mind. She knew from her long association with Simon that the compulsion to tell these stories was partly competitive: Simon had heard the story during those minutes she'd spent in the bathroom. He needed to remind her that he'd been on the scene when she'd been elsewhere. No doubt Simon had once suffered from a parent who tantalized, who kept the door open on scenes better left unspied upon. Perhaps—though she resisted this thought—he had excitedly imagined her in the bathroom, primping. In fact she had spent some minutes staring into the mirror and wondering how she could get through the evening without slapping someone. Mindy's cackle had set her off, Kath remembered. But she couldn't reconstruct the details. All she recalled was that Mindy had made an unfunny joke, something about the dead presidents at the back of the bar.

Kath turned, too quickly, and in her haste jostled a woman nearby who was wearing a lot of makeup over her tan. Apologizing, Kath darted away, down the vitamin aisle. It was getting hard to breathe. Maybe she was losing her mind, misplacing it the way she might her keys or her phone. She had to *contain* Stolz's story, even as it congealed inside her like hot jam in a jar.

The aisle wasn't quite deserted: a girl sitting at a card table was carefully filling plastic cups with bright yellow juice.

The juice, the girl said portentously, of the ancient and venerable sea buckthorn. Try some.

Kath selected a cup, sniffed its contents.

It tastes better than it smells, the girl assured her. She was fresh-faced with smooth, plump skin of astonishing clarity. She looked familiar. Kath couldn't place her.

Genghis Khan made his soldiers drink it. It's full of antioxidants.

The stuff slid down Kath's throat: cold, bitter, but not, for all that, undrinkable. The plastic cup felt oily against her lips.

What do you think?

It tastes character-building.

The girl laughed. She had good teeth, well-spaced and regular.

The juice was expensive. Kathy took a bottle anyway. She was stirred up.

She was in the parking lot when the insight came: She'd always felt a bit left out among that lot, the residents. Simon had stimulated her envy by retelling that story in the office as if she'd not even been *at* the pub. Admittedly, she'd ceded the field by visiting the bathroom, but surely, that was no reason to punish her. In other words, it was standard Simon behavior. He was a monster at bridge, snide about small errors. She hated to play opposite him, knowing she'd have to hear all about every hand she might have played differently. Was an inference to be drawn?

Something was *wrong* with Stolz's story.

JUICE-PUSHING'S JUST A SIDELINE. So's waitressing at the ex-presidents bar. Dorinda does her real work here at the nursing home. She doesn't get paid, not yet. She's just a volunteer. But she knows it's the work she's meant to do because she struggles just to show up. The work puts an important strain on her, her teacher says. Her body arrives at the job before she does, and it will sometimes be fifteen or twenty minutes before she feels herself click into place, a tumbler turning somewhere within. Sometimes she doesn't arrive at all, and on those days, she can't make her body and her mind line up. The tumbler doesn't turn; the pins don't get a chance to click. Her teacher says: That's how you know.

She clings to her teacher's faith. That he only teaches yoga doesn't matter. It's his presence in her life that makes the difference. At the nursing home she feels like she's stuck in a vat of vanilla pudding: vanilla walls, vanilla sheets, vanilla protein drink for the patients who can't be trusted to chew, which is to say, most of them. It's dull work, vanilla work, pushing the cart down the vanilla-colored hall and back again, doling out one cup at a time, waiting for the patient to drink its contents, taking the empty cup, marking the sheet: who swallowed, who didn't. The television blares in most rooms. Slack faces watch, eyes tracking slow. Dorinda believes people don't understand this kind of living—the lessened pitch, all colors greatly faded. Vanilla-ed. Occasionally while with a patient she catches a flash of the person who'd once fully inhabited that flesh and knew what it meant to have a memory, to have had the experience of having seen someone before. Since she herself needs so much more experience, she's inclined to patience. She'll apply to medical school someday. She doesn't have the grades but grades aren't everything. She wants to specialize in geriatrics or suicidology. She's interested in forms of life just this side of dying. Try putting that in a personal statement.

She stops outside the old doctor's room. 4B. He's in the armchair, wrapped in his dressing gown, slippers on his feet. The room has an echoing quality that makes it peaceful when television is off, which it usually is. He doesn't like television. He likes staring out the window.

Doctor.

His face contorts as he struggles to recall her name. Finally, he says: Dorinda.

She responds with a puppy's wide-mouthed smile. She can't help it. What she feels for him is hard to explain.

She's been told he's a psychiatrist. Aren't they supposed to be intuitive?

You wouldn't know it to look at me, would you, the doctor says, as if he'd heard her thought.

Wouldn't know what?

She hands him the cup. He swallows, grimacing. He's obedient.

That's awful, he tells her.

I know, she says.

You know.

He says it gently, so she feels the blade. Which she does, every time—even that one time, when the gangly middle-aged dude with the beer gut and the whisky breath had come to visit and she was on her guard with both of them. She's supposed to be on her guard at all times. But she isn't. She likes this patient's feisty quality, how he mocks and flirts, insulting her so she can't feel like she knows everything. She doesn't know everything. Maybe she doesn't know anything.

That's why I'm going to medical school, she adds. To know.

We have to *stop*, he tells her. That's what he said to Whisky Breath, too. *We have to stop.*

Another staffer might call him agitated. But his statement has a lively quality, consistent with his smoking jacket and wry flirtatiousness. It doesn't have the dully repetitive quality of a perseveration. He's trying to hit the right note, she thinks. It must be like trying to make a shot in tennis. You keep at it until you hear the ball against the sweet spot and then you know.

See you tomorrow, she says as she takes her leave. Looking back from the doorway, she sees that he's already gone, staring out the window again at the empty service road.

When she returns with the cart, the station nurse asks wearily: Did something happen?

In 4B, she adds.

A charmer, that one. Was he aggressive?

Dorinda takes the cups, one by one, and throws them in the trash, leaving the doctor's cup for last, the pale dregs still in it. She looks behind. No one is watching. She lifts the cup to her mouth.

STANLEY REMEMBERS so little now. But he still remembers the excitement of early July, when the university vouchsafed to him another litter of first-year residents. Always they were eager to please him and not anywhere near as eager to exercise restraint with their patients. Oh, how they resented the outpatient ward where they interviewed mere neurotics whose problems, they more or less secretly felt, could be resolved through the application of a little willpower. They saw those patients as inferior to the more exotic pathologies inhabiting the locked wards on the upper floors, where they, those greenhorns, preferred to be.

They needed time on the locked wards themselves, Stanley caught himself thinking. Then they would see how far their ideas about will and power would get them. They would be improved by such done time. But there was no wishing for that. Sadism went around like the flu. He'd figured out how to use that energy: he'd created a whole pedagogy and even—*quelle horreur*—won a teaching award. How they'd bristle at the tasks he assigned: yes, by all means, take a history, but submit it to me in the form of a sonnet. *A sonnet?* He'd smile and nod, all innocence. Talk about will and power. He'd edit the results, make them read aloud. He'd interrupt: That's where the line should break. Does it? Break? Just there? They'd blush, stutter. Now and then he'd get a weeper. The sting of humiliation was meant to take some of the starch out of them, so they wouldn't sting, or starch, a patient. That was the idea, to protect. Wounding them in this small way would make them more sensitive to the wounds of others.

Or so he hoped. How easily he fooled them all, not least himself. He was getting it back now, though. Take that tool, Jack Stolz, who even now had to mock him, projecting death wishes ("You have to stop") and threats ("chemical restraint"). But wasn't restraint always the watchword? Soon the nurse will arrive with her syringe full of euphemism. He won't fight. No sarcasm, no stink-eye. He'd just float. He'd remember what he could—the girl who was falling to pieces, the woman who planted spoons in her lawn, the therapist who adopted a patient—all gone now but for peculiarities that fixed these people in his mind, seemingly forever. He'd remember how evenly to suspend his attention; he'd try to imagine what life was like for that candy striper. Not the way he might have imagined her once, not the old luscious fantasy, but as she might actually want to be imagined. Although he can do very little for anyone in his present, diminished state, he can still dream. And while he can, he will.

THEY GATHERED AGAIN for Stanley's service—a memorial, since he'd been cremated—at a church that, despite its age and historic significance, displayed exactly zero ex-presidents in its windows. There was no beer, either—although Stolz, swaying in the pulpit as he delivered his eulogy, seemed to have made do, nipping from a flask he slipped in and out of a pocket while everyone pretended not to notice. Simon was sitting with Mindy, folding and refolding the paper on which he'd scrawled notes for the dull eulogy he'd just delivered. He suspected Stanley had planned the whole affair in the days after his diagnosis, before the dementia could interfere with his desire to control everything. The event had an overly rigid quality, even with Stolz nattering drunkenly on. How little control he seemed to have over his long arms and legs. Thank heaven it would be over soon. Rory would give a speech, Kath would read what Stanley's wife had prepared, they'd attend the catered luncheon for as long as Stolz could stand upright, and then they'd adjourn to the ex-presidents' bar. In fact, Simon was looking forward to it.

Seated in a pew across the central aisle, Kath was slightly masked, her face obscured by a large-brimmed straw hat that matched her suit: tropical wool in a bruised purple that was almost black, a color he felt as a rebuke. He'd offended her somehow, in recent weeks. Perhaps they'd make it up tonight. King hadn't made it; bad weather tied him up in Tampa. Rory wasn't showing well and perhaps should not have come, either: he looked like he'd been stuffed into his shirt, already the armpits were dark, and he kept running a finger under his tie—a pointless gesture, as he could no more loosen his necktie than he could slacken his grip on his own identity. Identity: In the end it was nothing more than the armored bunker in which they had all entombed themselves, gladly for the most part. Or so it seemed to Simon.

The last benediction given, Stanley's family filed out ahead of the congregation, which had risen as a body. The first and second wives, with their children and stepchildren, spurted up the center aisle, making no eye contact, exchanging no greetings, as if they, too, were ready to move on to some more special and bearable after-party, some ex-presidents' pub of their own. Following them, Stolz managed to trip over his own feet and go sprawling down the aisle before popping up again—thank heaven—like a tweed-coated jack-in-the-box. Simon stepped out next, offering an arm to Mindy as she picked her way down the pew. She scowled, pulling her shawl around her, and surprised them both by stumbling into his arms. *Christ*, she muttered and huffed off. He trailed behind, breathing urgently by numbers. Was it so necessary to have a hissy fit now, in front of his colleagues? As if to prove the point Stanley was forever making about relationships—how, no sooner had the bride and groom sworn to love, honor and protect, the one would move too fast or too slow for the other on the way up the aisle, and the stranger within would show its talon and snarl, as one of Simon's patients, a poet, had once put it.

He found Mindy outside the coatroom. He could tell from her gestures and tightened expression that she was speaking angrily about the gathering, insulting his friends no doubt. But he couldn't hear anything above the band, which had started up a gospel number. The Dixieland horns mocked the solemnity of the architecture, too clever by half. It was sheer Stanley. Yet something *had* changed: What should have irritated today only caused Simon to brim with tenderness. What a teacher Stanley was, what a magician! And what a miracle Mindy seemed to him then, still standing patiently by, sticking with him despite his faults. Bending to her ear, he whispered, What did you call them, my love?

Oh, when the saints—

The Honor Roll

"WHAT HAPPENED?"

For some minutes Craig had paced the kitchen, the tension of all he could not say evident in the small muscles around his mouth. He could not speak; he needed badly to speak. His tie roamed loose around his neck. "Where's Tonya?"

"At the library. She has one of those stupid group projects." Zinnia shuffled the pile of chemistry homework she'd been correcting. Push, don't push—she was never sure how to handle Craig in these moments. Push, she decided. "*What happened?*"

"Oh, Christ." He filled a glass with water from the tap. "I quit the PTA."

"You did what?" He was well-liked, respected.

"It was either quit or be tossed out. I took the path of least resistance." He passed a hand over his face. "No one wants an honor roll."

He'd been defending it since the end of the previous school year, taking an unpopular position against an increasingly vocal parental faction. Now, for his pains, he'd been pushed out.

"Was Geri there?" Geri, the school psychologist, agreed with Craig on this matter. She was also the mother of

Alexis, who had made Tonya's life miserable for the past eighteen months.

"She wasn't there. Her vote would have helped."

So, the group had moved without Geri. In her absence they must have sensed an opportunity. Craig opened a window, and the kitchen filled with loamy sub-divisional night air. Past watered lawns the river was lined with shuttered businesses—a print works, a textile mill, a tombstone grinder. They anchored memories of better times, boom times. She went to Craig, embraced him. He hugged back, slackly, and brushed a stray fragment of paper from her hair.

IN THIRD PERIOD, Zinnia yanked the cord for the projector screen and it snapped backward, out of reach. To retrieve it, she had to climb on a chair. It wobbled beneath her, and she grabbed the whiteboard's ledge to break her fall. The ledge came off in her hand.

On with the lesson, she told herself. On we go. Onward.

"Hydrogen bonds are weak," Zinnia said over titters. She set the broken item—light, aluminum—on the floor and waited for the hubbub to subside. "They only show up after the hydrogen molecule is already covalently bonded."

Here and there, an eyebrow arched into what might become a question, if only Zinnia could wait for it. Of course, she couldn't wait for it. The basic elements of her classroom had not changed in twenty years. Her impatience. Her awkwardness. The brine shrimp massed in their glass box, whirling around the aquarium's sole furnishing, a plastic monkey's head with glowing fluorescent teeth, a gift from a student. She was an anxious teacher, prone to mishaps and misstatements, a teacher to whom students gave ambiguous gifts.

A student raised a hand. His notebook was opened to a page as fresh and unmarked as his face. "What's the point of a hydrogen bond, then? It seems kind of—"

"Superfluous," said the girl with the strong PSAT verbal score.

"We could say that hydrogen bonds are like love interests," Zinnia tried again, doubling down in the hope of redeeming her initial error which, she now saw, was to talk about bonding with teenagers, "who are already married to someone else."

"So the marriage bond is a covalent one?"

In the tank, the monkey flashed his teeth.

"I'm not sure how far I'd push the metaphor."

The bell rang; her students scurried out. These were good kids, attentive and industrious. They weren't to blame for her classroom performance.

Their mid-year scores, a trial run for the AP test in the spring, had been disappointing.

THE NEWS ABOUT THE HONOR ROLL passed into the papers and from there into the kitchens and living rooms of Maple Bay. At school the phones would not stop ringing as parents who could not be bothered to attend PTA meetings—that is, most of them—registered their shock and anger. Albert, the principal, issued an all-faculty SOS, and the teachers gathered in the staff room.

"We tried to warn you," Geri said to Albert, who just wanted everyone to get along.

Albert waved his hands as if to say, *Whatcanyaddoo?* It was a habit that, out of earshot, once prompted Geri to sneer that Albert was a *gestural communicator*. But Zinnia didn't mind the way his voice stayed in her head.

Leonard, the music teacher, cranked open a window. "I don't buy it, Al," he said, through a pout refined by decades of after-work trumpet gigs. "Must be a slow news day."

Through the window Zinnia had an unobstructed view of the parking lot. The seniors with early dismissal loitered on the sidewalk, entranced by their phones. A news van rolled up and parked beside a formidably hair-sprayed woman checking her makeup in a clamshell mirror; a technician handed her a microphone marked with a logo that matched the one on the van. So the honor roll story would be on the evening broadcast, too.

Tonya slipped through the crowd. Her lemon-yellow backpack was smaller than the ones her friends carried. She was a lot like the backpack: neat, smart, bright. Precisely the same qualities Alexis had targeted for mockery months ago, at the start of what Zinnia privately called the Bully Year.

IT HAD BEEN MONTHS since the fight, and Zinnia still didn't know exactly what caused it. Rumors had circulated online, that much was clear, taking on weight and speed until they coalesced into a thrown punch that brought the Hallway A teachers running. When the bell rang, the bystanders slunk back into their classrooms, leaving Alexis and Tonya circling each other, snarling obscenities of the genus *cunt-bitch-slut*.

Later, in Albert's office, Alexis denied everything and refused to hand over her phone. She railed against Albert, her teachers, the whole idea of school. Geri patted her arm, and Alexis swatted Geri's hand away. *"Mom."*

On the sofa across the room, Tonya sat sullen-faced with arms crossed. Zinnia, feeling tense herself, decided to let her be.

"Look at her," Alexis sneered, "trying not to ugly cry."

Albert sighed through his nose. "I know it can be hard when your mother works at your school," he said. "You *both* know how hard that is."

This conciliatory move, a statement of what the girls had in common, elicited nods from the mothers and a derisive snort from Alexis. When Zinnia reached for Tonya's hand, Tonya flashed her a warning glance. She really was trying not to cry.

"Someone has to be the grown-up here," Tonya sniffled. "Alexis, I apologize."

Attagirl, Zinnia thought.

Alexis mimicked her. "*Someone has to be the grown-up here.*"

Zinnia's eyes stung. But Tonya, calmer now, only said, "My point."

"Bitch slut cunt," replied Alexis.

Geri snapped, "*Girls.*"

Albert assigned each girl one hour of detention before suspending both sentences. "On your personal recognizance," he said. "You're both good girls, and everyone knows this. But if it happens again—" With a finger he drew a line across his pouched neck.

After school, Leonard poked his head into Zinnia's classroom. She was holding a scoop-net full of dead brine shrimp. Perhaps twenty corpses lay in the net. Culled for some reason.

"What happened?"

"I don't know."

"I mean with Alexis?"

"I don't know!" She felt her face contort and squeezed her eyes shut, remembering Alexis's taunt. *Ugly cry.*

"Darkness hates light," Leonard consoled her.

But there was no darkness. There were only people making choices.

"You can't punch down," Leonard said in his soothing tenor. "It is what it is."

Years ago, when she was still a student, Leonard cajoled her out of the practice room, convinced her to join the marching band. He called her *sweetheart,* and the endearment made her pliant, willing to do after-class favors like collecting scattered sheet music and straightening chairs. Other girls did *more,* she'd heard; the baton squad girls were rumored to be particular favorites. Zinnia played her flute at football games and in the Presidents' Day parade, all the while wondering why she'd not been chosen for *more.*

Eventually she stopped wondering. Any shy flautist would easily feel inadequate compared to a baton squad girl who danced down the football field in high boots and a miniskirt hiked to *there*. For all his nighttime gigging, Leonard was no bohemian. He talked in rote phrases; he liked girls who were conventionally attractive. Who could blame him for liking what everyone liked?

But—*sweetheart?*

Amazing what you could get away with saying, then and now, so long as you said it like Leonard.

OF COURSE ALEXIS was having trouble. Alexis was always having trouble. This surprised people who only saw the bright hair and Hollywood teeth, a look that Tonya, riffing on a new coffeehouse product, dubbed "flat white." True, Alexis was at the top of the food chain socially—prom queen, homecoming queen, queen of the girls who droned around her, tapping their glitter-crusted fingernails against the screens of their phones. But Alexis had flunked chemistry and algebra. She bombed the SATs. She bombed the ACTs. This year she might even flunk statistics, which no one ever flunked. Something was wrong with the way she was wired, the teachers agreed privately. But the consensus was held closely, not shared around and certainly not with Geri.

"You can't say hey, someone hit your kid with the idiot stick," Albert remarked to Zinnia, taking her aside one afternoon in the middle of the Bully Year. Of course, that's pretty much what Tonya had told Alexis, or so she suspected. Probably not in so many words. But kids knew. They always knew. In the hall they flowed past like the shrimp in her tank.

"You certainly can't say that to a colleague," Zinnia replied. "To anyone, really."

AMONG THE MANY THINGS not under parental control, the most tendentious was class composition. To minimize mutinies, Geri had for some years led an activity designed "to give parents more insight into the process of sorting students into ability groups," as she explained in her annual email.

The activity was simple enough. During a series of group parent-teacher meetings, attendees collaboratively sorted their children into such "ability groups." The result was a "first draft," as Geri put it, of the following year's rosters. Teachers reserved the right to reassign students. According to Geri, including parents from the start could stave off challenges later on. As these challenges were frequently referred to the guidance office, it made sense that she should lead the charge.

The meetings always started well. Parents just off work cheerfully helped each other out of suit jackets. Ties were loosened, pumps kicked off. Stirrers swirled in cups of coffee—decaf, given the lateness of the hour. Such nice people, these well-intentioned parents who loved their children. Then the knives came out.

While some parents feared their children were behind, others talked hopefully of Harvard and Yale. The worriers considered these speculations unfair. College was still so far off. Brilliance might yet descend on a student, if not a sympathetic division-one coach. Anxieties mounted. Conflict simmered. At a certain point, someone had to be blamed, and the target was inevitably a teacher or administrator, someone outside the family unit.

Year after year, Geri had stayed scrupulously neutral. But this winter—just when, Zinnia could not help noticing, the composition of their daughters' class would be decided—Geri began to favor one side of the debate. It wasn't that Geri was generally against ability grouping. But for the first time she objected to particular decisions, wondering if this or that student were truly "up to" the challenges of Algebra Two or AP U.S. History. Her murmured doubts tended to derail the meetings. Yet for all that Geri disapproved of ability grouping, she'd said not a single word in favor of the abolition of the honor roll. Zinnia couldn't figure it out.

Neither could anyone else. The shift in Geri's stance set the rest of the faculty to whispers and, in Zinnia's case, soul-searching. One night soon after Geri began raising questions, Zinnia declared herself. "Ability groups are unfair. Not every student comes from a home where parents help with homework."

"Not to mention other, more expensive forms of support," Geri agreed.

"Now I know all of the *bleeding hearts* will call me a *hard ass*." Albert paused to shoot a hard look at Zinnia. "But the truth is that if you remove disruptive students from the classroom, group kids according to ability, and stay the hell out of the teacher's way, kids will learn!"

Although this straight talk—well, it *sounded* like straight talk—earned murmurs of agreement from the parents, a few tensed as if waiting for the counterattack. Once you were branded a bleeding heart, there was no undoing the taint. Zinnia had no idea why Albert had selected her to play the scapegoat.

Then again, Tonya had been selected for a similar role. She'd been up-tracked routinely, too. Had one caused the other? A smart girl was easily branded a freak.

Hatch, the chair of the English department, said, "Rendering all the students equally mediocre creates a crowd in which weaker students are allowed to hide."

"So it's really more of a herd thing?" asked the biology teacher, a petite woman taking time off from her PhD. It was her second year at the school. Possibly her last. Zinnia recognized the signs. Injection of irrelevancies at meetings was one of them.

Leonard said, "Without the honor roll, all the students are now equally mediocre as far as any outsider can tell."

"Outsiders being?" Hatch prompted, fishing his watch from his pocket.

"College admissions officers, for one thing," Albert said. "The gatekeepers."

"Once upon a time, we prepared some kids for professions and careers." Leonard was in good form tonight, tanned and glowing from his work with the baton squad, which was practicing outdoors now that the weather had improved. "And we prepared the rest, who were the majority, for jobs that no longer exist. Now we have to pretend they're all going to college because the reality is too unbearable. The military's all they've got. That and jail."

A silence like after a wreck.

"Don't you go all bleeding-heart on me, too, Leonard," said Albert.

"Jail!" Geri jammed her papers into her tote. "Talk about tracking."

She slammed out. The door hit the frame with a noise like a shot.

"Jesus," Leonard muttered. "Take the wheel."

Zinnia soothed herself with geometry, imagining distances and angles. But molecular bombardment was also a geometric science, and the results of fission were pretty loud. The real problem was, no one ever expected Geri to erupt at a meeting. No one expected that much violence from a flat white.

Rustlings followed: a scraped chair, a cleared throat. They weren't supposed to fight in front of the parents.

"It's getting late," Hatch observed.

Albert shut his leather folder. "Class dismissed."

They filed out quietly. Passing her own darkened classroom, Zinnia was only slightly cheered by its shining surfaces, the brine shrimp whirling in the tank.

ZINNIA FIDDLED with her calculator, double-checking a grade. The temptation to nudge the numbers up was worse this year. In the days since the botched meeting, Geri had gone off the rails, canceling meetings with some students and referring others to outside experts—psychologists, nutritionists, learning specialists. Turfing kids was unusual for Geri, who prided herself on working with all comers. Zinnia felt somehow responsible for her distress.

Years before, in high school, Geri had been part of a pretty-girl clique. They came late and left early, skipping classes in favor of going on dates with men who offered expensive jewelry but weren't always so forthcoming about their marital status. In those days Zinnia felt ugly and uncouth in Geri's presence, as if she half-agreed that grades, scores, advanced degrees and the security to which they supposedly led were nothing more than another form of vanity, of self-indulgence. Had anything changed since then?

Zinnia didn't like to think of Tonya as an emissary for her own biases, but she feared that Alexis had looped Tonya into a fight for which she was unprepared precisely because she was, like Zinnia, nerdy and achievement-oriented, not into gossip, clothes, and hair.

Geri had her own story, of course. Zinnia knew its outlines well enough to wonder, on good days, about Geri's hastened transition to adulthood, so unlike her own.

THAT WEEKEND, Zinnia and Craig were invited to Albert's annual faculty party, which always included the year's seniors and their parents as well. Tonya begged off, citing homework. Zinnia wasn't sure she wanted to go either, given the circumstances, but Craig insisted. "He's depending on us."

"And we've *been* dependable. We can afford to skip a year."

Craig wound his scarf around his neck. "Not this year."

"Well, then, what's the plan? Make nice, pretend every-thing is fine?" Zinnia zipped her jacket and swiped her lips with ChapStick. "Everything is *not* fine, Craig."

"You need to calm down, Zinnia."

Hah, she thought. *Famous last words.*

At the party, the kids stayed outside, hunting for Easter chocolates. Albert's wife had been up at dawn, tucking Cadbury eggs and Hershey kisses into inevitably soggy nooks in the backyard. Inside, someone had placed a box of matzo on the dining room table beside a basket of tiny foil-wrapped chocolate bunnies. Albert handed Zinnia a flute of prosecco.

"There's someone you should meet," he said. This wasn't strictly true—there was no one at this party whom she *should* meet, it was not that sort of party—but Albert liked to settle his guests into conversations, and he expected teachers to put the parents at ease. He introduced Zinnia to a middle-aged couple. The husband wore a cardigan and driving mocs; the wife, yoga pants and a baseball cap. They seemed familiar but Zinnia struggled to place them. Was their child in Honors Chem?

The conversation shifted through variations on the theme of domestic management. There was a complex family schedule, much ado about equipment going in and out of the minivan. The couple finished each other's sentences. They seemed like a single organism, a big, sporty self.

"We're a soccer family," the wife explained, leaning into her husband's arm. "Our schedule's so crazy I don't even have time to do my hair."

"Did you know," Albert said, addressing himself to Zinnia, "this lovely lady," he gestured toward the woman in the baseball cap, "has a lovely little girl who just got into Williams!"

Ah. Zinnia had heard of this girl. Soccer goalie, fantastic athlete. Not in Honors Chem.

"Here's to your daughter." Zinnia lifted her flute. The woman smiled thinly. Her husband shook his head. She'd made a misstep, praising the student apart from the mother.

Oh, these parties.

"Williams! For soccer!" Zinnia griped to Craig afterward, on the street. Why should she praise what she did not admire? "You would think she got into *Harvard*. On *smarts*."

"Don't punch down," Craig reminded her.

They passed a parked minivan crammed with sports equipment. Zinnia lifted one arm high and brought it down, hard, on the windshield. Cracks radiated from a single point, a hexagon of nothing. Zinnia leapt back, fist wrapped tight around her elbow, which throbbed in its depths. "I'll punch where I want to," she gasped, surprised to find that this was true.

"Jesus, Zinnia." Craig threw an arm around her and hurried her away.

THE OUTBURST HAD FEW CONSEQUENCES. Craig offered ibuprofen and ice. Tonya had seemed unmoved by the barebones version of events they relayed to her, but then, out of the breezy blue, she called the television station and demanded to be interviewed about the honor roll debacle. On the first official day of spring break, a van topped with a satellite dish pulled up to the house. Tonya ran out, followed by Zinnia who, her bad arm tucked in a sling, staked a position near the door. It was a windy day. In the flowerbed, the daffodils whipped to and fro.

"What will you do without the honor roll?" The reporter thrust the microphone at Tonya's face.

"It's not really about me." Tonya jutted her chin over her scarf. When she spoke, she sounded like Craig, reasonable, politic, open-minded—the grown-up in the room. "Our parents and teachers made this decision for us. The students were not consulted. If a decision affects you, shouldn't it include you?"

Zinnia retreated into the house. Tonya was right, of course. No one had asked the kids to weigh in. The whole mess was only about the parents—what they wanted, who they thought they were, who they imagined their kids to be. That last one, especially.

Between bouts of grading Zinnia interspersed manipulations of her elbow, recommended by a medical web site to preserve the range of motion, and in these empty painful minutes, she kept returning to the woman in the ball cap. What had motherhood been like for her? Zinnia imagined years of after-school parties and late-morning coffee klatsches in homes selected with one eye on the school district and the other on the retirement fund.

Later, poking around Geri's Facebook archive, Zinnia found expectable things: photos of a kitchen renovation, of a trip to Six Flags. Geri was a working mother, Zinnia remembered. Like Zinnia, she would have been unable to make those coffee klatsches, either.

Zinnia shut her laptop and, with difficulty, set the kettle to boil. Doing everything one-handed was proving a challenge. She'd overfilled the kettle, and now it was too heavy to lift with her bum elbow.

THERE WAS SOMETHING ABOUT LINOLEUM, Zinnia thought, the reassuring noise it made against chairs that scraped, shoes that slipped. Here she was again, at yet another faculty meeting devoted to the honor roll. To "process our loss" as Geri had written in an all-staff email invitation. "I want the opportunity to explain what the honor roll meant to me." No one had the heart to refuse.

Albert checked his watch. The biology teacher disappeared into her lesson planner. Geri crossed her legs, opened her notebook, and exhaled deeply. "My father *died*," she began. "Six months later, *so did my mother*."

There was Albert, egg on his tie; Hatch, fiddling with his pocket square.

"There was no counseling, there was no coddling." Geri's voice grew clipped. "I was living with my grandparents. I was failing school. My big sister gave me a dollar for every A I got. She didn't know what else to do. That's how I made the honor roll."

Zinnia remembered this sister, her sturdy walk, the way she held her binder canted off one hip as she walked down the corridor, the forgiving linoleum dappled with light. It was so easy to tender a hopeless judgment: Your child will travel *this* road and not *that* one. But the honor roll was different. Aspirational.

The sister had gone to a fancy college, Zinnia recalled. What had become of her?

"Your sister—"

"She could *deal*," Geri snapped at Zinnia, "but she couldn't feel."

In the great rotary of their lives, feelers had the right of way. "Okay, Geri."

"Besides, I'm talking about *me*. When I saw my name in the paper, I was so incredibly proud." She paused and Zinnia felt the catch in her own throat. "I wanted to do it again and again. I wanted to show everyone that I wasn't going to end up *in the gutter* just because I didn't have a mom or a dad anymore."

"Oh, Geri," Leonard said. *Oh, sweetheart.* "You worked hard. You did all the extra-credits. You got to know your teachers. They were proud of you. We all were."

"You changed my life, Leonard." Her eyes were wet. "*You.* This dumb *school*."

The tableau seemed so complete Zinnia nearly forgot that she was part of it. Dumb or not, dumb *and* not, the school could still be a place of miracles, even if only small and dirty ones. In class that day, her tallest Honors Chem student had stunned her by offering to pull down the screen so she could project the periodic table onto it. Another volunteered to clean the shrimp tank. Zinnia peeked at Leonard, at Hatch—their patient, caring faces had not changed in decades.

Leonard whispered, *How's that arm?*

Acknowledgments

Several stories in this collection first appeared in *Conjunctions, The Saint Ann's Review, Folio, Verity La,* and *Sou'Wester.* "Alberto: A Case History" won the SLS/Fence Prize in 2005 and was subsequently published in *Fence.* "Psoriasis Memoir," which won the fourth Fictionline Prize, was available online until 2003 at Fictionline.com, a pioneering writer-funded organization founded in 1999 by Scott Southwick; the story was subsequently published in *Tartts Seven,* edited by Joe Taylor. I'm grateful to all involved with these publications, particularly their editors.

A few sentences in "The Radio" are adapted from Douglas Kahn and Gregory Whitehead, eds., *The Wireless Imagination: Sound, Radio and the Avant-Garde* (MIT Press, 1994).

Finally, I'm deeply grateful to my team at Cornerstone Press: Brett Hill for his keen editorial eye, Abby Paulsen for her striking cover, and Sam Bjork and Sophie McPherson for their help with sales and media. Thank you as well to Dr. Ross K. Tangedal, Cornerstone's visionary director and publisher, whose patience, wit, and grace are exceeded only by his commitment to his students as champions and stewards of twenty-first century American literature.

Diane Josefowicz is the author of a novel, *Ready, Set, Oh* (2022) and a novella, *L'Air du Temps (1985)* (2024). Her short fiction has appeared in many national and regional publications including the *Conjunctions, Sou'Wester, Fence, Saint Ann's Review, Dame, Folio, Verity La,* and elsewhere. She is books editor at *Necessary Fiction*, senior editor for translation at *The Adroit Journal*, and managing editor of the *Victorian Web*, the internet's oldest and largest website devoted to Victoriana.

She holds an MFA in fiction from Columbia University, a PhD in the history of science from MIT, and a BA from Brown University in Providence, Rhode Island, where she lives with her family.

www.ingramcontent.com/pod-product-compliance
Lightning Source LLC
Chambersburg PA
CBHW031045310726
48969CB00007B/2132